# A MARRIAGE OF NECESSITY
# THE RULES OF REFINEMENT

## THE MARRIAGE MAKER BOOK EIGHT

## TARAH SCOTT

ISBN-13: 978-1-953100-31-3

www.scarsdalepublishing.com

Cover design by dreams2media

Editor Casey Yager

First Trade Paperback Printing by Scarsdale Publishing 2018

10 9 8 7 6 5 4 3 2



SP

# RULES OF REFINEMENT

Noblemen aren't always honorable... but a rake is always charming

In a narrow lane off Edinburgh's illustrious Charlotte Square, stands a town house that is not quite as impressive as nearby residences, but remains a place of distinction. An air of quiet dignity is maintained by the courtyard that fronts the street, while privacy is assured by a wrought-iron gateway. This house is Lady Peddington's School for Young Ladies and is owned and run by Lady Honoria Peddington.

Girls fortunate enough to attend the academy are instructed in all aspects of proper comportment with emphasis on the importance of a pleasing demeanor and appearance, grace and good manners, the skills a lady needs to run a large, well-to-do household, and – of course - the necessity and advantages of an impeccable reputation. Scandal, the girls are warned, must be avoided at all costs.

Lady Peddington's own reputation is the finest, and all Edinburgh considers her above reproach. She is especially well-loved by the affluent merchants and lesser gentry who live on the fringes of the city's New Town where she operates her school. These clients appreciate her knack at finding affluent husbands for their daughters. No one suspects that her knowledge of men comes from the long-ago days when she wasn't Lady Honoria Peddington, but simply Honey Pedding who ran a well-doing Glasgow brothel.

Those skills, though secret, still serve her well, for when her school's famed graduation balls fail to secure suitable husbands for some of her more high-spirited girls, other gentlemen come to the fore, eager to accept these gems as pampered mistresses. So, however a girl's heart might lean, Lady Peddington's School for Young Ladies guarantees happiness for all.

# CHAPTER 1

ANNE ANGLED AWAY FROM HER BEST FRIEND, JEANINE, DREW back the edge of her glove, and glanced at the face of the silver gilded watch pinned to the inside of the fabric. 11:57. If her watch was correct, and the time piece had kept perfect time for three generations, the third ball of the season would end in three minutes when the minuet concluded. Then Lady Peddington's famed Midnight Ball would begin.

A year of her life, along with funds her family could ill afford to lose, gone. All for nothing, if she didn't find a wealthy husband by the next ball, which was one short week away. Her heart constricted. *Oh, papa, why didn't you tell us?*

She knew why. Her father had been a Weber male through and through. They were stubborn to a fault, determined to care for their own at all costs, and slaves to the gambling halls. In the end, he had the presence of mind to lay down his cards before he lost the castle on Loch Lomond, and the estate and land north of Perth. Her father, however, feared he couldn't resist the temptation to gamble away their remaining holdings and drank himself to death.

The need to cry rushed to the surface.

Nae, the time for despair was long past. She had to—

A tall, dark, good-looking gentleman approached. Anne's mind snapped to attention. Two minutes remained of the respectable ball. It was impossible to join in the dance so late in the set, but would this gentleman engage her in conversation? He continued toward them. Anne turned her attention to Jeanine. It wouldn't do for her to appear too eager.

"I am so glad this ball is almost over," Jeanine said. "I met an interesting gentleman earlier. He's older—though not old enough for my purposes." She sighed. "It is so hot and stuffy in here. I think there are more guests tonight than last week. I wonder if there will be even more for the final ball of the season next week."

From the corner of her eye, Anne watched the man's approach. He brushed past a group of men.

"Aye, it is warm tonight," Anne said to Jeanine. "We can go back to our rooms together, if ye like."

The man reached them, and she and Jeanine faced him. He looked at Anne. Her pulse jumped. Finally, a gentleman was going to speak with her. He would be the first of the evening.

Then his attention shifted to Jeanine. "Would ye honor me with a turn around the ballroom?"

Tears stung Anne's eyes. She ducked her head as Jeanine said, "I am tired. But Lady Anne is free. Why don't you walk with her?"

Anne snapped her head up in time to see the man stiffen. "I beg your pardon, but it is getting late," he said. "I must be going. Have a good evening." He started to turn.

"Wait," Jeanine cried. The man stopped, interest lighting his eyes. "Why won't you walk with Anne?" Jeanine demanded.

"Jeanine," Anne hissed under her breath, and she glanced at a group of nearby ladies who were frowning in their direction. But Jeanine ignored her.

"Do you know that she's the heir to a title?" Jeanine asked.

"I have no need of a title," he said, and before they could reply, he spun and strode away.

Jeanine faced her. "I am certain of it. Linda and Dorothy are speaking badly about you. Fiona, too, I wager," she added in a dark tone.

"Why would they?" Anne said. "What can they possibly say that would alienate these gentlemen? And why say anything at all? There are plenty of gentlemen seeking ladies."

"Because the gentlemen fawned all over you that first night," Jeanine said. "You're more beautiful than any other lady here."

That, Anne knew, was untrue. There were some very beautiful girls here. Jeanine was one. But leave it to Jeanine to be loyal to a fault. Still, something was wrong, and Anne couldn't escape the feeling that the girls Jeanine had named did have something to do with it.

The lights began to dim. Her heart fell. The respectable ball had ended. Anne spotted half a dozen servants weaving throughout the ballroom and snuffing out candles. They would extinguish more than half the candles, leaving the massive room with many shadows.

"It's time to leave," Jeanine said.

Anxiety knotted Anne's stomach. Once she left the party, she would have to wait another week for the opportunity to find a suitable match. There had to be some way to prepare for the next week. She couldn't sit passively in Lady Peddington's parlor and sew, sip tea, and talk about the final upcoming ball. Even if she met a gentleman tonight or next week, what guarantee was there she would make a match? She couldn't wait to the last minute and simply hope to find a husband. The candles on the table behind them were snuffed, leaving them standing in soft shadows.

Jeanine tugged on her arm. "Come along, Anne."

Dare she stay? Anne scanned the ballroom. At least one

hundred and fifty guests, including Lady Peddington's girls, had attended the night's ball. Half of those had left. Anne counted ten graduates of Lady Peddington's School for Young ladies amongst the guests. Some had even removed their gloves. Three girls stood far too close to gentlemen, and the orchestra struck up a waltz. The Midnight Ball had officially begun.

Two gentlemen looked their way.

"Oh dear," Jeanine whispered. "Two gentlemen are headed our way. If we hurry, we can avoid them."

Anne faced Jeanine. "Quickly, you go on. I'll be up later."

"Nae, you need a husband with money," Jeanine's whisper grew urgent. "These men can offer you nothing."

Jeanine might not be correct. Some courtesans received very expensive gifts. Might she receive enough expensive gifts to support her estate for the next three years? Her mother had a good head for business. She could manage the tenants while Anne earned the money it would take to plant and harvest three years of crops. After that, Dover Hall could support itself *and* Castle Dòmnallach.

But that required substantial money…

The two gentlemen reached them and stopped closer than propriety allowed. But then, this was the Midnight Ball. Propriety had exited along with all the proper ladies.

The gentleman who stopped in front of Jeanine gave a slight bow. "May I have the honor of this dance?"

Jeanine glanced at Anne.

"Go on up to your room," Anne said. "I will be up later." She glimpsed the satisfied gleam in the eyes of the man standing near her.

"Just one dance, my dear," Jeanine's admirer urged.

Jeanine narrowed her eyes on Anne. "If you're staying, then I am staying." She looked at the gentleman. "I am happy to dance with you."

Before Anne could object, Jeanine slipped her hand into the crook of the man's arm and allowed him to lead her toward the dance floor.

Anne hesitated. She should go after her. Oh, this was a terrible mess.

"Would you care for a walk in the garden, love?"

Anne looked sharply at the man standing uncomfortably close. She had no experience with men who were seeking mistresses, but she had been the object of male attention since the age of fourteen. Six years was long enough to gain some understanding of male passions. Only twice before had a gentleman referred to her with a personal endearment—outside of her father, of course. The first, was the boy she fell in love with at sixteen. They fell out of love a year later, but remained friends to this day. The other time mirrored tonight. The intimacy hadn't been earned, and evoked a sense of uneasiness that made her skin crawl.

Was this how a courtesan felt? Could she give the most private part of herself to a man who viewed her as nothing more than an object to serve his pleasure? Memories rose of her mother sitting before the hearth at Dover Hall, sewing on a cool autumn evening and her sister, Louisa, racing into the room with a drawing to show them or a passage from a favorite book she wanted to share, and the answer was a resounding yes.

But did that mean a walk in the garden?

Once they reached the cover of darkness, what would stop this man from taking what he wanted and then not paying for her charms? She flushed hot at her thoughts, but shoved aside the shame. How did a courtesan go about getting a man to offer a contract? The answer came more easily than she liked. She must tease just enough to entice him to offer a contract—a good contract.

Anne slanted her head and looked up at the man through

her lashes. "Perhaps, sir, it would be better if we began with a dance. A walk in the gardens might be something for people who are on more…intimate terms."

A corner of his mouth lifted, and dread seeped through her. "My dear, I have no qualms about counting myself among the fortunate number of your lovers, but I have no intention of being the man who finances them."

Anne blinked. "I-I beg your pardon?" Her thoughts whirled. Finances *them*? She drew a sharp breath. "You think that I am looking for a protector and want to take lovers at his expense?"

He leaned closer and she stiffened when he traced a finger up her arm. "After we have enjoyed ourselves, I *might* introduce ye to a man who will look the other way when you take lovers while under his protection."

Her mind cleared. "You believe I will trade my-my—for a—" Words failed as fury clouded her thinking. She arched a brow. "A walk in the garden, you say? You like the dark, sir?"

"Like it?" he said with a growl. "I prefer it."

Men were fools.

This time, she met his gaze squarely. "In my experience, a man who prefers the cover of darkness to make love to a woman is a man who is lacking in the proper—" she gave him a cool smile "—*tools* to please a lady."

He blinked, then his mouth thinned. "The gentlemen you draw into your web are most fortunate."

She lifted her chin. "You will not count yourself amongst their ranks."

It seemed he would say more, but he spun on his heel and strode away.

Anne released a deep breath, then realized a nearby group of men were staring. God help her, by tomorrow, word will have spread through Edinburgh that one of Lady Peddington's graduates was available for the taking.

"You can't fully blame him, you know," drawled a deep male voice behind her.

Anne whirled to face the speaker, a tall man leaning against the wall. Good heavens, he was handsome. The blue eyes that started at her were made all the more blue by his raven dark hair.

"I beg your pardon?" she said.

"There is no denying that Niall is uncouth," he said. "But you can't fault him for speaking the truth."

The temper that had got her into far too much trouble over the course of her life—including just a moment ago—reared its ugly head once again. "You know nothing of the situation."

"Unlike Niall, I respect a woman who knows what she wants and isn't afraid to pursue it," he said without rancor.

She frowned. "What the devil are you talking about?"

"A woman has just as much right to pursue her pleasure as does a man," he said.

Then she understood. "Where did you get the idea that I'm seeking lovers?" She should have known better than to stay for the Midnight Ball.

"Are ye saying it isn't true?" he asked, but before she could answer, he added. "It seems to be a well-known fact."

"Something can be a fact only if it's true," she said with exasperation.

He laughed. "You just rejected Niall's advances by telling him that you won't add him to your list of lovers."

She gave a frustrated shake of her head. "I was angry."

He laughed. "There is no need to be coy. I meant what I said, I respect a woman who isn't afraid to go after what she wants."

Anne exhaled a breath in an effort to control her temper. "But you insist that what I want is a string of lovers. What in heaven would I do with them?"

He pushed away from the wall. "Perhaps I can be of help in demonstrating the benefits of having at least one lover."

She rolled her eyes. "That would completely undermine my plans."

"What might those plans be?"

"I fail to see how that is any of your business," she said.

He shrugged. "If I'm to help, I must know your plans."

"Help?" Anne narrowed her eyes. "If you intend to help in the same fashion as that other gentleman, no thank you."

"I would never be so uncouth," he said.

A twinge of hope surfaced.

"Niall should never have asked you to trade your charms for the possibility of introducing you to a man who might be interested in becoming your protector."

"What should he have done?" she asked cautiously.

The man took two steps closer and grasped her hand. The warmth of his fingers caught her off guard. Eyes locked with hers, he lifted her hand and brushed his lips across her fingers, then released her.

"A lady should always know what to expect from a gentleman."

Anne agreed completely.

"A woman as beautiful as you should expect nothing less than a diamond bracelet after an intimate evening."

She stiffened. He didn't intend to make her his mistress. He intended to have her for one night, then send her home. *With a diamond bracelet*, her mind whispered. The situation had grown far more desperate than she could have imagined. Not only had she failed to capture the interest of a suitable prospect for a husband, she couldn't even interest a man in making her his mistress.

It made no sense. Men had vied for her attention—many, for her hand in marriage—since she'd turned sixteen. Now that she *needed* to marry, she was avoided. Quite a few men had approached her at Lady Peddington's first ball—or, at least the first half of the ball, now that she thought about it.

"Good heavens," she said under her breath. Jeanine was right. Someone had spread rumors about her. She regarded the gentleman. "Where did ye hear these things about me?"

"Men talk—just as women do, I wager."

"How dare they," she muttered.

"I beg your pardon?"

"They've ruined my chances of finding the right man."

"Perhaps I am the right man," he said.

She surveyed him, his raven hair, blue eyes, broad shoulders and long legs, then shook her head. "Nae, you are too handsome."

He blinked. "I had no idea being 'too handsome' was a drawback."

"It is for my purposes."

"I promise you, my dear, it isn't."

She gave a frustrated shake of her head. "A man like you has no need of a mistress, much less a wife."

His expression remained impassive. "Are those the only choices?"

She narrowed her eyes. "There you have it. I am correct. You are looking for a woman who will entertain you for an evening and then leave her with some silly trinket."

"I assure you, I never give 'silly trinkets' to ladies."

Nervous laughter emanated from somewhere in the shadows to Anne's right, but she kept her attention on the man. "How expensive is the jewelry that you would give?"

He lifted a brow. "Are we negotiating?"

Anne suddenly felt certain the conversation was going all wrong for a courtesan searching for a protector. Still, she said, "Call it curiosity."

Amusement appeared in his eyes. "Just the other day, I happened to see a particularly lovely gold bracelet and was saddened by the fact that I had no one to give it to. The bracelet would cost me two hundred pounds."

That meant she might sell it for one hundred pounds, if she were lucky. Her stomach knotted tighter. A man and woman glided past them.

Anne shook her head. "Such a small gift would do me no good."

His gaze sharpened. "What would do you some good?"

She waved him off. "I have no time to waste when you are offering me a bauble for my trouble."

"Trouble?" he repeated, then laughed again, this time full, rich and with amusement.

To her horror, warmth rippled through her. He stepped closer. So close, she caught a whiff of the sandlewood soap he'd used to bathe. But unlike Niall, he made no move to touch her, and her desire to step back wasn't out of revulsion, but a desire to hide the blush that warmed her cheeks. Good Lord, the man was charming.

"I promise ye, my lady, that you will not consider a night with me 'trouble.'"

The spell broke. Anne narrowed her eyes. "I see, I am to consider myself fortunate to have a night with you, and grateful for the bonus of a gold bracelet."

"I don't think that's quite what I said."

"It is exactly what you said," she retorted. "It's the height of arrogance for a man to think that a woman should thank him for bedding her."

His expression cooled. "I believe it is you who *asked* me to thank you with a gold bracelet."

She drew a sharp breath. He was right. Still… "Aye, but you act as if some of that payment should come in the form of gratitude for being fortunate enough to be chosen for your one night of-of…" she was at a loss for words.

"*Affaire d'amour?*" he drawled.

She snorted. "One night can hardly be called an affair and has nothing whatsoever to do with love."

"Is that what you want, my lady, love?"

"A woman always wants love. Well, love doesn't put food on the table." She read the surprise in his eyes and realized she'd lost control of the situation. "Take yourself off to some other woman who is willing to sell herself for a gold bracelet," she said. "I have business to attend to."

KENNEDY DOUGLAS, VISCOUNT BUCHANAN, ENTERED HIS STUDY and the erotic fantasy of the ravishing beauty at Lady Peddington's ball lying on his sheets beneath him vanished at sight of his stepmother seated on the divan near the window. She sat straight—the proper wife—her honey-brown hair swept off her shoulders in a carefully coiffured mound atop her head. Her ivory evening dress, befitting a thirty-year-old woman, hugged her trim, perfect curves. Too bad her husband had one foot in the grave.

"What fresh hell has brought you here at this time of night, Jacqueline?"

"I realize it is after one in the morning," she said, "but I have been waiting since nine."

He had indulged a little too much in the free-flowing champagne at the ball, but the presence of his father's wife in his study at one forty-five in the morning dictated that he have something stronger than champagne to drink. He crossed to the sideboard where sat half a dozen decanters filled with various liquors, and poured himself a liberal dose of scotch. He put the top back on the decanter, picked up the glass, and turned.

He leaned against the sideboard. "Short of forcibly throwing you out, I suppose I can't stop you from telling me what the earl wants. Unless, that is, I simply retire to my bedchambers." Kennedy sipped his scotch and watched her over the edge of the glass. "Would you be bold enough to follow me, if I did?"

"I am here on an errand for your father, nothing more," she replied.

"Of course. You won't risk him questioning your faithlessness with his death so close at hand."

"Really, Kennedy. Must you always be so cruel?"

He gave her a cold smile. "With you, my sweet, I am afraid so. I know I'll regret asking, but what is so important that you waited nearly five hours to tell me? I know it isn't that my father is dead, for you would have hazarded the gates of hell to find me, if that were the case." He took another drink of whisky. The pleasant burn comforted. "Not to mention, you're not smiling."

"It really is unkind of you to continue to imply that I will be happy when your father dies."

"As I said, with you, there is no other way. What do you want?"

She reached into her reticule, withdrew a piece of paper, and looked up at him. "This is from your father."

He gave a mirthless laugh. "You could've left that on my desk. Better yet, you could have sent it by messenger. Why are you here?"

"Since you refuse to see your father, he sent me with this message, and instructed me to wait for a reply."

Kennedy finished the scotch and turned to refill the glass. "As I have no desire to see my father, what could induce me to read his letter?"

She sighed, then the rustling of a paper followed, and she said, "Kennedy, I imagine you will not deign to touch a paper that I have touched. No matter. If you force Jaqueline to read this, it will be all the worse for you. I am dying. But you know that."

Kennedy poured a double dose of liquor.

"I have commanded you to marry," Jacqueline went on, "but you go about your business as if you have no responsibility to me, the title, or our position in society. I believe that you have not married—will not marry—just to spite me. But I cannot allow your vendetta to bring an end to our line. I know threats of cutting you off from my money are meaningless. You would rather live in squalor than do a single thing I ask. Therefore, you leave me no choice."

Kennedy slowed in sliding the decanter top back on the decanter.

"You will marry within the week" –Kennedy released the decanter top as she finished the sentence— "or I will marry your sister to Lord Granbury ten days from now on her sixteenth birthday."

Kennedy whirled. "What the bloody hell?"

Jacqueline said, "There is more. 'You might think to make off with your sister and hide her somewhere, which is why I have already sent her away. No one save myself knows where she is. If I die tomorrow, no one will know where to look for her.'"

Kennedy stared. "This is insanity."

Jacqueline didn't shift her eyes from the letter, but continued, "I will not settle for a betrothal. You must marry and produce an heir within a year. Do so, and I will allow you to choose your sister's husband when the time comes. Defy me, and I will not only marry her and Granbury, but they shall not return home until she has produced an heir for him."

Kennedy dashed his glass against the hearth and took two steps toward Jacqueline. "This reeks of your handiwork."

She shook her head. "You underestimate your father, and overestimate my influence."

"I know you both too well to mistake either of you," he snarled.

"What possible reason could I have for wanting to see you married?" She dropped her gaze. "I had always hoped…" She raised her head, eyes shimmering with moisture.

"By God," he exploded, "you missed your calling. You should have been an actress. Pray, do not pretend you have any tender feelings for me. Those illusions were shattered the day you rose from my bed and announced your engagement to my father." He snorted in derision. "I suppose I should thank him for marrying you. Though had he any idea that he was saving me from making the greatest mistake of my life, I'm sure he wouldn't have done it."

A tear slipped down her cheek.

Rage rammed through him. He crossed the room, seized her wrist and yanked her to her feet. "Where is Rose?"

She shrank back and shook her head. "I don't know. As the letter states, only he knows. He wouldn't chance my telling you." More tears slid down her cheeks. "He knows that you and I are close."

Kennedy released her and staggered back two paces. "Of course, he knows. That's why he married you."

She shook her head. "Nae, he does not know that we were —" She broke off

"Lovers?" he sneered.

"We were much more than that." She took a step toward him.

He turned away, his steps faltering, and reached his desk in time to brace himself, his back to her. "Leave, Jacqueline."

"Please, Kennedy, we cannot leave things like this between us."

"There is no *us*," he said.

Her skirts rustled and he realized she was walking toward him. He whirled to find her three steps away. He had to get away from her. Kennedy strode to the door. Hand on the knob, he looked back at her. "I suggest you not return home to your husband for at least an hour."

Half an hour later, Kennedy banged on the door of his father's mansion. The door opened in two seconds. Somewhere in the recesses of his mind, he realized the footman had been waiting for him. He pushed past the man and raced up the stairs to his father's bedchamber. The door stood open. Aye, his father expected him. He continued inside and found his father propped up in bed. A fission of alarm shot through him at sight of his father's yellow pallor. He looked far worse than when Kennedy had last seen him a year ago. Cruel fate. Only an hour ago, he would have rejoiced in seeing his father's decline. Now, until Rose was safely home, his father's illness frightened him more than anything ever had in his life.

The earl laid aside the book he'd been reading and met Kennedy's gaze.

"Where is she?" Kennedy demanded.

"Once you are married—to a proper lady, mind you, no peasant from the country—and once you produce an heir, I will bring her home," he replied in a strong voice that belied his appearance.

Kennedy's hands worked into fists at his sides. "I will kill you for this."

"Then you will never find your sister."

"She is not a child. She can find her way home." But she was a child. Only fifteen.

His father's gaze remained locked with his. "Do you really think I would make it that easy?"

Rage threatened to overwhelm him. His thoughts jumbled. His sister, only fifteen years old, being held prisoner somewhere. Would her jailers safeguard her?

Kennedy swayed. "How do I know she is safe?"

"She will always be safe under my care," his father replied.

"Your threat to marry her to Granbury proves otherwise," he snarled. "You know full well he beat his first wife to death."

"You are intelligent enough to know that gossip rarely resembles true events," the earl replied.

"I'm intelligent enough to know that most gossip has some grain of truth to it. If one hair on her head is harmed, I will kill you."

"You're threatening a dying man, Kennedy. I have made peace with my imminent death."

"You could live another year, to three or four. I can end you before that. I can end you tonight."

"Then you would never see your sister again."

"What happens if you die before I can produce an heir?" His heart thundered.

"I suggest you pray that doesn't happen."

Kennedy stared. His father was a bastard, but this went beyond anything Kennedy could have imagined the old man capable of. "You cannot keep her prisoner forever. She will escape. She will return home. Your threat is unreasonable." The last, he said more for himself than his father.

"Your sister isn't in Scotland. Escape is nigh to impossible. Even if she did manage by some miracle to escape, she would have to journey home. She has no friends, no money, no escort." The last words were said with an emphasis that told Kennedy his father knew the exact picture that had arisen in Kennedy's mind at the thought of his young sister trying to return home on her own. And she would try just that.

"You would sacrifice your daughter?" he whispered. "Risk her losing everything, possibly even her life, just to force me to marry?"

"You see my actions as those of a man bent on hurting you. I see my actions as those of a desperate man trying to preserve his legacy."

"Legacy?" Kennedy sneered. "I should have known. This has

nothing to do with me. You don't give a damn if I marry or even carry on the title. This is about you wanting to be *remembered*." Kennedy released a harsh breath. "If you wanted to extract revenge because I had Jacqueline before you did, I would have more respect for you. But this—" He shook his head. "You are right. These are the actions of a desperate man. You're a liar, Father. You do fear death." His father's eyes narrowed, but Kennedy gave him no chance to reply. "I will marry within a week. But on one condition."

His father waited.

"Once you confirm my wife is with child, you will bring Rose home."

His father shook his head. "Your wife could lose the child, and the child might not be a male. I know you well enough to know that you wouldn't touch her again just to spite me."

Kennedy stared. "I would agree to the terms, if I were you. Keep in mind, I have considerable resources at my disposal. You know, of course, the moment I leave this house, I will begin my own search for Rose. If fortune favors me—and she often does—and I find my sister before you die, I will divorce my wife and immediately set about siring a string of bastards, none of whom can claim your title." Kennedy gave him a cold smile. "Then I will seduce your wife and sire a child on her that cannot possibly inherit your title."

His father's eyes widened. "You're not capable of such dastardly actions."

Kennedy gave him a cold smile. "I am capable of far worse. After all, I am your son."

# CHAPTER 2

THE FOLLOWING MORNING, KENNEDY HAD JUST CALLED FOR HIS carriage when a footman announced the arrival of a guest, Sir Stirling James. Kennedy frowned. What was the marquess doing here so early, and without an appointment?

"Show him in," he said.

Moments later, the footman reappeared and announced Sir Stirling James. Kennedy rose, circled his desk and extended a hand toward Sir Stirling. They clasped hands.

"Forgive the intrusion," Sir Stirling said, and released him.

Kennedy indicated the chairs and divan hear the window. Stirling took the seat and Kennedy sat on the divan.

"It's no intrusion," Kennedy said. "What can I do for you this morning."

"I believe it is what I can do for you," Sir Stirling replied. "I understand you need a wife—immediately."

Kennedy blinked. "How the devil do you know that?"

Stirling flashed white teeth. "The news appeared in this morning's gossip sheets."

"I wouldn't take you for a man to read gossip sheets," Kennedy said.

Stirling's smile didn't falter. "A man needn't read the gossip sheets for news of this magnitude to reach him."

"How the bloody hell did the news get out so quickly?" Kennedy muttered. Then instantly knew the answer. Not only had his father known that he would show up in his home last night, he had known Kennedy would capitulate.

That made no difference.

Kennedy refocused on Stirling. "Forgive me, but I have important business this morning. I was on my way out when you arrived."

"No doubt on your way to propose to whichever lady it is you've chosen to marry."

The man was uncannily perceptive. But, then, perhaps it wasn't that hard to guess. Or was it? Kennedy regarded him. "The fact that I'm on the hunt for a wife in no way indicates that I'm racing to the altar. Yet, I get the impression that's what you think."

"You must marry within one week, if I understand correctly."

Kennedy started. "Surely that wasn't in the gossip sheets?" That would ruin him.

Sir Stirling shook his head. "Forgive me, nae. *Society* only believes that you have decided to marry. However, I understand that your father gave you a week to marry."

Anger surged through him. "My lord, you and I are not well acquainted. Forgive me, but how the hell do you know that?"

"The best I can say, is that servants talk."

Kennedy cursed. "What has any of this to do with you?" His mind raced. He knew Sir Stirling only casually. He wouldn't have pegged the man for someone who engaged in idle gossip, or who took advantage of those in a vulnerable position. But he'd been wrong about men—and women —before.

"It is well known that you have no interest in marriage," Sir

Stirling said. "To my knowledge, there is no one particular lady that you favor."

"What of it?" Kennedy demanded.

"I assume, that you would choose a lady among your acquaintances to fulfill your father's demands. However, I know a lady who I believe will suit your purposes quite well."

Kennedy was at a loss as to how to reply. Of all the things this man might say, this had never entered his mind. He sat down. "How is it you know someone who will suit my needs?"

"Pure luck, I assure you. This is a lady who is in need of a husband with money."

Kennedy barked a laugh. "That is a qualification that could include half the women in Edinburgh."

Stirling nodded. "True. However, this is a lady who is sure to satisfy your father in a way most other ladies cannot. It's an obvious conclusion to say that your father would like you to carry on the title. However, the earl strikes me as the sort of man who would like to leave behind, shall we say, a legacy."

Kennedy gave a slow nod. "Your information is uncannily accurate."

A smile tugged at Sir Stirling's mouth. "This is more of an impression than information I have gleaned. I don't know your father well. In fact, I've met him but twice, and the last time I saw him was five years ago at a soirée in London. He is a man who is certain of his place in the world, and the impression he will leave behind."

"You almost make him sound noble."

"He's your father, and I would not speak ill of—"

"I have no illusions as to what sort of man my father is," Kennedy cut in.

Stirling gave a slow nod. "He cares a great deal about how he is viewed by the world. By you and your son carrying on his title, he believes part of him will live on. That is not an unnatural feeling. However, he might consider your successes and even your son's successes to be a result of his actions."

"It's more than that," Kennedy said more to himself than Stirling. "Even now, with one foot in the grave, he can't stand to have *Society* view him as weak. He must be the ever-constant force that keeps the world in motion."

Stirling smiled, and Kennedy was surprised at the compassion he read in the man's eyes. "What a shame that he's wasted his life on meaningless pursuits, instead of caring for the one person whose world did revolve around him, if only for a little while."

Kennedy felt as if he'd been punched in the gut. What tiny bit of love that had remained after his father tore him from his mother's deathbed and sent him to university a year ahead of schedule, he'd killed when he'd married Jacqueline. Kennedy barely remembered the days when he'd worshiped his father. Yet those feelings cut like a knife.

"Of course, your father assumes you will choose from the pool of ladies with whom you are acquainted."

Kennedy realized Stirling was speaking. "What? Oh, yes, I must marry a woman of breeding. He was very clear on that point."

"This lady will fulfill that qualification. She is, in fact, Viscountess Kinsely, heir to the title. Her father died with no male heir."

"A second title in the bargain," Kennedy murmured. "You are correct, that would please my father."

"It would please him even more if he thought the idea was his," Stirling said.

Kennedy frowned. "What do you mean?

"I mean, if your father decided who you should marry..." His words trailed off and he shrugged.

In truth, Kennedy was surprised his father hadn't chosen

his bride. "How will my father come to this conclusion?" he asked.

Stirling grinned. "Leave that to me."

"I can take no chances," Kennedy said.

"Of course not." Stirling rose. "I would guess that you'll hear from your father by tomorrow."

Kennedy stood. "How do you plan on making him think this was his idea?"

Stirling shrugged. "Very simple, really. All that must happen is for him to learn of the lady's existence. He will be unable to refrain from interfering."

THE CARRIAGE SLOWED, AND ANNE CAUGHT SIGHT OF A MASSIVE stone mansion through the window. She had to be dreaming. The last two nights she'd lain awake searching for a plan that would save her home and her family. Nothing short of ten thousand pounds would ensure they had a chance at survival. Two hours ago, she'd received a note. A summons, really. The Earl of Buchanan requested—commanded—her appearance at his home at three for the purpose of… Despite the presence of the maid sitting across from her, Anne couldn't help pulling the note from her reticule and reading it for the hundredth time. *…arrange a betrothal between you and my son, Viscount Buchanan.*

A hundred questions swirled inside her head. Why couldn't his son find a wife? Why did the Earl want to marry *her* to his son? How had the Earl heard of her? She was the daughter of an impoverished viscount who didn't move in *Society*. She couldn't remember the last time her father had visited Edinburgh. Had the Earl not heard the terrible rumors about her? Maybe he had, but his son couldn't get anyone better than an unfaithful woman. Her head felt near to bursting with questions.

The coach tipped slightly and in the next instance, the door opened. Anne extended her hand and allowed the footman to help her to the ground, then he helped her companion. Lady Peddington had insisted the maid accompany her. In truth, Anne was glad for her presence, even if her companion couldn't offer any advice.

The footman closed the coach door and Anne nodded her thanks, then walked with the maid up the walkway to the door. She knocked. A moment later, the door opened and a footman led them to a large parlor where they settled on a divan. Anne's heart began to pound and her hands sweated inside her gloves. She had not the slightest idea what to expect. How she wished Lady Peddington had come with her, but other duties prohibited her from accompanying Anne.

The door opened and a short, thin man entered. Anne rose and Molly followed her example.

"I am Mr. Spector, my lady." He bowed. "His lordship's solicitor."

Anne looked past him at the open door.

"His lordship will not be here," he said. "He is very ill. I represent his interests."

Anne nodded. "Oh, forgive me. This is Molly, my companion," she said.

Mr. Spector bowed again, and said, "Please, be seated."

They resumed their seats on the divan and Mr. Spector took the chair to Anne's left.

"As I said, his lordship is ill. He wishes his son to marry post haste." The man gave what, Anne assumed, was meant to be a comforting smile, but it looked more pained than comforting. "He is willing to offer you a generous settlement."

Anne's heart pounded. She had known this topic would arise, but had assumed that by the time it did, she would be on intimate enough terms with her prospective husband for him to understand that her title would be her dowry. But a man in line for an earldom had no need of a title as viscount.

"Sir, perhaps his lordship is unaware that I have no dowry to offer, other than the title that will pass to my future husband."

Again, the man offered a smile, this one almost a grimace. "Indeed, my lady, the earl is well aware you have no dowry. He is pleased that his son will carry your title. If you will take a moment and review the contract." He pulled a document from an inside jacket pocket, unfolded it, and handed it to her.

Anne angled her head in thanks, and began reading. When she'd finished, she was more than certain she was dreaming. The earl would settle five thousand pounds on her on the day they married—which would be two days hence—and another ten thousand pounds the day she bore his son an heir. On top of that, she would receive a thousand pounds a year to do with as she pleased. The five thousand pounds was enough to get them through the first harvest season.

Her thoughts threatened to churn into chaos, but she forced order and concentrated on one thing: the money. There was no guarantee she would bear a son the first year. A thousand pounds a year wouldn't support the estate, but another fifteen hundred would get them by. As the wife of a wealthy viscount who was heir to an earldom, there had to be a way for her to get more money. But how? Never mind. She would figure that out along the way. She couldn't possibly get a better offer than this one.

She looked at Mr. Spector. "I own property north of Perth as well as in the Highlands. That property will remain in my possession."

"I believe that will be acceptable, my lady. So long as the property falls to your son at your death."

She nodded. "My mother and sister live at Dover Hall. They will remain there as long as they wish."

He nodded. "You will reside here in Edinburgh until you bear an heir. After that, you may retire to the country, if you wish. Of course, your son will remain here in Edinburgh."

A chill swept through her. Leave her son? She hadn't considered that. But then, she hadn't considered children beyond the knowledge that children were an obvious result of marriage.

"Are you saying, I will be banished to the country while my children remain here in Edinburgh?"

"Nae, my lady. I am saying that you would not be allowed to leave your husband and take them to the country."

"Not even for a visit?"

"Of course, you and your husband may decide to visit anywhere you like. But the children will be raised here in Edinburgh."

Her heart sank. She hadn't given a thought to where her children might be raised, but upon reflection, she couldn't imagine them being raised anywhere but at Dover Hall. This was far more complicated than she'd considered. But then, like now, she had considered only the money. What a fool she'd been to think she could simply marry a man and live life as she chose. She had to marry, of that there was no question. But her life would no longer be her own. She could visit Dover Hall and Marr Castle, but even that was dependent upon her husband's goodwill.

What choice had she? At best, she her sister and their mother would last one more year before the creditors swooped down upon them. If that happened, none of them would have a home.

# CHAPTER 3

ANNE HALF WISHED SHE'D INSISTED UPON MEETING HER FUTURE husband at the church rather than agree to wait at Lady Peddington's for his carriage. Whether he picked up her and her family from Lady Peddington's and rode with them to the church, or met them at the church, there was no turning back.

Her sister fidgeted beside her on the couch in the parlor, and her mother sat in the chair to their right, gripping a handkerchief, as they awaited the viscount's carriage.

"You look so terribly pale," Anne's sister said.

Anne gave Louisa a smile. "Nerves, nothing more. Once the ceremony is over and we're all settled into our new life, things will be just fine."

"I know it makes no difference, but I still want to say once more that I wish you hadn't done this," Louisa said. "We would have found another way. That nice Mr. Allen has been courting Mama. A marriage proposal is sure to come any day."

"Mr. Allen is a nice man," their mother said, "but he has no money to speak of."

"Between us three and him, we could have found a way," Louisa insisted.

Anne smiled. The determination and hope of youth. Only a year ago, she had been full of that same optimism.

"I've made a good match," Anne said. "He's the heir to an earldom—a very wealthy earldom. We need never again worry about money."

"Only if he gives ye enough money to help us keep Dover Hall running," Louisa said. "Not to mention, Castle Dòmnallach."

"Two years from now, the estates will be self-sufficient," Anne said. She would see to that. "You and Mama need never worry about having a home. You will have time to make a good match, Louisa, and Mama can marry whomever she likes, whether or not he has the skills necessary to run the estates. We shall stay in control of our property."

"Dover Hall will go to your son," Louisa said.

"Only upon my death," Anne said. But Castle Dòmnallach will remain yours."

At the thump of boot falls in the corridor, Anne snapped her attention toward the parlor door. Her heart began to pound.

*Steady*, she told herself. *Mama and Louisa are here. You do not want them to see you frightened.*

The boot falls came closer. Her mother's and sister's attentions were also fixed on the open door. Closer. He would be here any second.

Anne tore her gaze from the doorway, reached for Louisa's hand and squeezed gently. Louisa's head snapped in her direction.

"Remember," Anne whispered, "this man will be your new brother. We must not make him uncomfortable."

Louisa nodded, but worry furrowed her brow. From the corner of her eye, Anne glimpsed movement in the doorway.

"Viscount Buchanan is here to see you, my lady," the butler announced.

Louisa's eyes widened. Their mother started to rise. Anne, still holding her sister's hand, pushed to her feet, pulling her sister up with her, and faced her future husband.

The butler stepped aside and Anne stared. In all her wildest dreams, she wouldn't have guessed that the man she was betrothed to was— "You," she whispered.

"Bloody hell," he muttered.

Their mother dropped into a courtesy. Louisa curtsied, pulling Anne down into a curtsy with her.

Anne straightened and extended her hand toward him. "It is a pleasure to meet you at last, my Lord."

Something flickered in his eyes. She realized she'd miscalculated, but didn't know how. He approached, grasped her hand with long fingers, and brushed his lips against her knuckles.

"I cannot tell ye how pleased I am to meet you, my lady."

He still gripped her hand. She tugged harder than she should've had to in order to free herself. She turned slightly. "May I present my sister, Lady Louisa, and my mother, the dowager viscountess."

The viscount bowed over both their hands, then said, "It is a pleasure to meet you."

"It was very kind of you to fetch us yourself, my lord," her mother said.

He gave her a polite smile. "It is my pleasure, and, please, ma'am, call me Kennedy."

Her mother angled her head in acquiescence and started to reply, when Dorothy and Fiona entered the room. They stopped short as if in surprise, and Dorothy's hand flew to her mouth.

"Oh my," Dorothy exclaimed. "We didn't realize this room was in use. Forgive the intrusion."

They realized it quite well, Anne wagered. The girls were

not typically in this part of the house at this time of day. But all the better.

Anne smiled. "It's no intrusion, Dorothy. Ladies, may I introduce Viscount Buchanan. My lord, this is Miss Williams and Miss Evans."

The girls curtsied and the viscount gave a slight bow.

"How wonderful to finally meet you, my lord," Linda said. "We didn't have the chance to meet you when you attended Lady Peddington's ball last week."

Anne stiffened. The little vipers thought they would expose her to her mother.

"Which ball would that be again?" the viscount said.

"Lady Peddington's ball, last Saturday evening," Dorothy said.

The viscount frowned as if in thought. "Ah, yes, I believe I did drop by, but arrived later than intended, during Lady Peddington's Midnight Ball."

Anne stared. Was he giving them a set down for trying to embarrass her?

The girl's faces turned ashen.

"Sir, you must be mistaken," Linda quickly said. "We did not attend the Midnight Ball."

His frown deepened. "Then perhaps it wasn't me you saw." He faced Anne and her family. "Forgive me, but we should leave if we are to reach the church on time." His gaze shifted to Anne. "Have you any trunks, my lady?"

"Nothing to take with us to the church, sir," she replied.

"And you are dressed for the ceremony?"

Her cheeks warmed. "Aye, sir. The lace is the finest in all of Scotland and the pink satin," she smiled, "pink is a favorite of mine."

"It is a stunning color on you," he said. "Shall we go?"

They nodded and he stood aside as they walked past Dorothy and Linda and proceeded him out of the room. He caught up to Anne and her heart thundered with the fear that he would mention their meeting at Lady Peddington's. He didn't, however, and he helped them into the carriage, and they started forward with a creak of the carriage wheels. Anne was all too aware of the heat from his body. He remained a perfect gentleman, but made no effort to sit far away from her on their side of the carriage. Was he was taunting her? Was he one of those men who needed a woman to stay close at his side?

"Do you live in Edinburgh?"

Anne started at the sound of Louisa's voice. To her surprise, the viscount smiled gently at Louisa. "A great deal of the time, aye. We have a castle in Inverness, which I used to visit every year."

"Not anymore?" she asked.

"Not as much as I'd like," he said. "Perhaps you will like to visit."

Louisa smiled. "Indeed, sir, I would."

He looked at Anne and her face heated. "Do you like Inverness, my lady?"

"I have never been."

"It's quite beautiful."

Had that been a wistful note in his voice?

"You and your family are welcome to spend as much time there as you like."

Anne's stomach knotted. Was he going to send them away? Mr. Spector said otherwise, but...

They reached the church and entered the foyer. Anne glimpsed only four people sitting in the pews before a young woman ushered her mother and sister into the chapel, leaving Anne alone in the foyer with the viscount.

"Very clever," he said in a low voice once they were out of earshot.

He didn't have to explain, she knew exactly what he meant. "I had no idea you were the man I met at Lady Peddington's ball," she said.

He gave a mirthless laugh. "The coincidence is too much of a, well, coincidence. I do no' believe you."

She let out a frustrated breath. "How could I possibly have arranged this? Your father contacted me. I never met him."

Doubt flickered in his eyes. "Do you know Sir Stirling James?" he demanded.

She frowned. "Who?"

"Never mind," he said. "I supposed it doesn't matter."

His tone said it did matter. The murmur of voices echoed back to them from the chapel. "When I saw you at the ball, you did not appear to be a man desperate to marry," she said.

"How does a man act who is desperate to marry?" he asked. "Any desire to marry had little to do with me being at that ball."

She snorted again. "That, I believe."

He gave her a critical look. "Your actions were not those of a woman interested in marriage."

"You're basing that on vicious gossip."

"Hardly. I am basing that on the fact that you negotiated with me for a night in your bed."

She lifted her brows. "I thought it was a night in *your* bed."

His mouth twitched in what she realized was amusement, but the mood vanished almost as quickly as it came. "Let me be very clear on one important point. You will take no lovers until I have an heir and a spare."

Fury whipped through her. "I assume the same rule does not apply to you?"

A cool smile spread across his face. "A man's by blows will never be mistaken for his heirs."

"Then the vows we are about to take mean nothing to you."

"On the contrary, they mean a great deal to me. You and our children will have my protection and my support."

"But not your loyalty," she retorted.

"Make no mistake, my lady, real loyalty takes place outside the bedroom."

THE PRIEST ENTERED THE FOYER, AND KENNEDY TURNED TO face him.

"If you are ready, my lord, my lady," he said.

Kennedy nodded and the priest returned to the chapel.

Kennedy looked at his wife-to-be. "Shall we? He winged his arm toward her.

She slipped her hand into the crook of his arm, then he led her into the sanctuary and up to the altar. Only half a dozen people sat in the pews, including Anne's sister and mother. His father's solicitor sat beside Jacqueline in the left front pew. Kennedy wouldn't be surprised to find her outside their bed chambers with her ear pressed against the door, so that she could confirm the consummation of the marriage. One other man sat in the third pew. Sir Stirling James. Stirling gave him an almost imperceptible nod as they passed. After the ceremony, Kennedy would speak with him. He wanted to know how Stirling knew of Anne—and got word to his father about her existence.

They reached the altar. Anne pulled her hand free and turned to face him.

Christ, he was about to marry a woman who only last week had bartered with him for her charms. She was lovely, there was no doubt about that, but he would have his father's head for this.

Kennedy weaved through the ceremony like a man in a dream. When the priest asked for the rings, Kennedy slipped onto her finger the diamond and ruby ring that had been his mother's. She put on his finger a simple gold band. That, he was surprised to admit, suited him well. The priest pronounced them man and wife and bade Kennedy kiss his wife. He slipped an arm around her slim waist and pulled her closer than intended. She clasped his shoulders and he glimpsed her closed eyes in the instant before his mouth touched hers.

As he knew they would be, her full lips were soft and warm. The embrace lasted by three heartbeats. She pulled back before he did, and the priest led them to the registry. They signed, but Kennedy felt no relief despite the fact he'd taken the first step toward fulfilling his father's demands. Unless his search for his sister succeeded, at least three months of hell lay before him, and that was only if he was able to impregnate his wife right away. What would he do if it turned out she was barren, or worse, he was unable to sire a child?

He couldn't help a rueful mental laugh. All these years, he'd been careful not to father a by-blow. If he had been careless—or lucky, depending on how one viewed the matter—

and had sired a bastard, at least he would know he was able to father a child.

Suddenly, his wife was being hugged by her mother and sister. He was forced to allow Jacqueline to kiss his cheek, and she did the same to Anne, her sister and mother. Mr. Spector shook hands with Kennedy. Kennedy looked back at the pews, but Sir Stirling was gone.

Forty-five minutes later, they sat at the dining table at his townhouse, partaking of the wedding feast. Kennedy would have gladly sent Jacqueline home, but here she sat to his left, while his wife sat to his right. He wasn't likely to forget this day for the rest of his life.

"Will you visit us at Dover Hall, my lord?" Lady Louisa asked him.

He looked up from his plate and smiled at her. "I beg you, call me Kennedy. We are family now, I am your brother."

She beamed. "Then ye must call me Louisa."

He nodded. "Thank you, Louisa. As to your question, we will plan a time to visit Dover Hall. For the moment, I have business that keeps me in Edinburgh. Of course, you and your mother are welcome to stay with us as long as you like."

"That is most kind of you," the dowager viscountess said. "Unfortunately, we must return home tomorrow." She smiled. "Like you, business beckons."

He wondered what business the dowager viscountess might have, but he would save that question for another day. "Of course, I understand."

"Perhaps we will be fortunate enough for your business to conclude in the not-too-distant future, so that you might come visit us," she said.

Kennedy had no intention of going anywhere until his son was born. But he smiled and said, "Perhaps."

"Anne can always come and visit us, as well," Louisa said.

Kennedy had no intention of allowing her to go anywhere until they had a son, but, again, he said, "Perhaps, though I may want to keep her to myself for just a little while."

That comment earned him a startled look from his wife. He didn't know her well—in truth, he didn't know her at all—but he had a suspicion that silence wasn't her normal state, and he wondered if he should be worried.

"Do you spend much time in Edinburgh, my lady?" Jacqueline asked the dowager viscountess.

"Nae, the running of Dover Hall demands most of my time."

Kennedy forked pheasant into this mouth. Was this the business she spoke of? The running of an estate could monopolize one's time.

"Surely you will spend more time here now that Anne and Kennedy are married. Are you certain you cannot stay another two days? We are planning a ball in their honor tomorrow evening."

Kennedy snapped his gaze onto Jacqueline. "I know nothing of this."

"Your father wanted it to be a surprise, and we had to be sure the preparations were in order before we said anything. I'm pleased to say that we have sent out two hundred invitations."

Kennedy thinned his lips. "It didn't occur to my father that we might have plans?"

She gave a gentle smile, a mother's smile, that would have fooled anyone except him. "Your father is not long for this world, Kennedy. Would you deny him something so simple?"

"It seems I cannot deny him anything."

Anne gave him a startled look and Kennedy realized she hadn't spoken a single word the entire breakfast.

Jacqueline laid a hand on his arm. "Kennedy, your father wanted me to tell you that he will be sending a wedding gift."

Anne's gaze flicked to Jacqueline's hand on his arm. Kennedy cursed inwardly. He had intended to keep his life separate from his marriage. Jacqueline, however, clearly had other ideas.

# CHAPTER 4

ANNE PULLED HER SHAWL CLOSER ABOUT HER SHOULDERS AND paced the carpet in front of her bedchamber's low burning hearth. She was a virgin, but she wasn't without knowledge of what transpired between a man and a woman. It wasn't that which had her on edge, however. Well, not totally, at any rate. Part of the problem—a large part of the problem—was that she found her husband attractive. It would be far easier for their marriage of convenience to remain a convenience and nothing more. To make matters worse, he believed she was a loose woman. But was that truly the worst part? She hadn't missed the way his stepmother laid her hand on his arm. The gesture was intimate, that of lovers. Surely her husband wasn't having an affair with his father's wife?

She stopped and plopped down on the chair in front of the hearth. Why hadn't she been fortunate enough to simply marry a short, pudgy man with bad breath? Instead, she married a man who could rival the gods. He clearly had no intention of being faithful to her—not that she'd ever given that much thought. But she would rather not be embroiled in a family drama that would land them in the gossip sheets. Had she married that short, pudgy man with bad breath, in all likelihood, he would have had little opportunity to be unfaithful.

She braced her elbows on her knees and rested her chin in her hands. She was an idiot. Any man with money could find a woman who would spread her legs for him. Why in God's name did she care? She had yet to consummate her marriage and already she worried about her husband taking a lover. No doubt, the viscount would have a string of women over the course of their marriage. She would save herself a great deal of grief by giving the matter no more thought. She only hoped his stepmother wasn't among those lovers.

What mattered now was the money she would receive upon producing an heir. That attempt would begin tonight. She wished she had a little time to become comfortable in her marriage before having a child. Even a marriage of convenience would take some time to grow accustomed to. But she had no more the luxury of time now than she had a week ago.

A knock sounded on the side door and she jumped. Good Lord, what was that? The door connecting her rooms to the master's chamber, she realized. Her heart began to beat fast. Another knock.

She stood. "Come in."

The door open and the viscount entered. He wore a silk robe cinched at the waist. Tanned flesh was visible in the V at his neck. He was even barefoot. Was he naked beneath the robe? She'd never been alone with a man in such a state of undress.

"Are your mother and sister settled in?" he said.

Anne nodded. "Yes, thank you. And thank you for having them here."

"This is now your home," he said. "They are welcome anytime."

She nodded, he said nothing, and she had the sense that he simply wanted to get the night over with. She recalled their conversation at Lady Peddington's ball—his implication that a night with him would be well spent. Oddly, he seemed to have lost that bravado.

"Why did your father choose me to marry you?" she asked.

He hesitated, then said, "He wanted your title."

Anne frowned. "Why would he want my title? He is an earl. My title is meaningless."

"But it isn't meaningless. It's another feather in his cap. He made a match for me that brought with it an elevated status in society."

"Your father is ill. Why would he possibly care about such things?"

He gave a mirthless laugh. "My father will care about such things from the grave. He has an insatiable desire for power and status."

"He would have you marry an impoverished woman just because you could take on the title of viscount?"

"My current title as Viscount Buchanen is courtesy, because I am his son. That is no longer the case. I am now Viscount Kinsley, and with that comes all the privilege and status, along with the property you own."

She tensed. "I informed your father's solicitor that the property that my father owned would remain mine. Dover Hall will go to our son, but Castle Dòmnallach will remain with my sister."

He nodded. "I have no intention of taking possession of your property. I'm only explaining to you my father's motivation. When my father dies, I will be the sixth Earl of Buchanen and Viscount Kinsley." He lifted a brow. "Very impressive, do you not agree?"

Anne noted sarcasm in his voice.

His expression grew speculative. "I explained why my father chose you. Now, explain why you agreed to marry me."

She shrugged. "I would think that should be obvious. I need money."

"That's why a two-hundred-pound bracelet wasn't worth the night with me," he said.

She nodded. There was no use pretending otherwise. "Your father is very anxious to have a grandson."

"So anxious, he would offer you five thousand pounds once one is born. That's a king's ransom compared to a paltry two-hundred-pound bracelet."

He almost sounded offended. "Our marriage is a business agreement," she said. "Would you prefer I wanted love?"

He grimaced and said, "God forbid," with such fervor that she wondered if she should be offended.

But she said, "Then you are in luck," with more emphasis than intended, and cursed her temper. "I have a family to care for. That is why I married you. You needed an heir—and your father wanted another title. A perfect match." She regarded him. "Why did you allow your father to choose your bride?"

"He wanted me married immediately and I had no preference."

"How sad," she murmured.

"Do you think so?" he said. "Should a man always be in love?"

Anne shook her head. This time she had offended him. "A man needn't be in love to have at least one friend he might be able to choose as a wife."

"Perhaps I take more seriously the task of choosing a wife than you did a husband."

"On the contrary, I put a great deal of thought into the sort of husband I need."

"Your only requirement is that he have enough money to support your ancestral homes."

Was he trying to make her angry? For once in her life, she couldn't be riled so easily. She gave a slow nod. "Aye, I had but one requirement: he must have money. But it seems you had no requirements."

"That is where you are mistaken, my sweet. My one requirement was that my father approved."

"Perhaps you and I are not so different," she said. "A man of your rank and wealth, would allow his father to choose his wife for only one reason. Did he threaten to cut you off?" She couldn't help but smile. "Have no fear, my lord. I admire a man who knows what he wants and isn't afraid to pursue it."

KENNEDY STARED AT HIS WIFE FOR A MOMENT IN SURPRISE, THEN threw back his head and laughed. "At least I will no' be bored with you, my dear." His amusement vanished. "Perhaps my father did me more of a good turn that I realized."

Her brows shot up. "Never say that is a complement, sir."

He chuckled. "A man must give due were due is deserved. I believe I might keep that to myself, however. My father need not know."

"When will I meet him?" she asked.

"Good God, never, if I have anything to say about it."

"Surely, he will want to meet me," she said.

"If he were a normal father, aye. But he isn't. He will want to see our son when he is born."

Her cheeks pinked prettily, and he realized they'd better get on with the business of the evening. She dark hair tumbled past her shoulders. He took the two steps to her side, then gently removed the shawl from her shoulders and tossed it aside. She wore a practical linen nightshift that didn't quite hide the rose-colored tips of her breasts. His cock began to rise. Aye, he would have no trouble bedding this woman. When he slipped an arm around her waist and pulled her close, she leaned away from him.

He looked down at her. "Husbands are often known to show their gratitude with jewelry."

Her mouth parted in surprise, then her eyes narrowed, and he realized his mistake. "How very kind of you to show your gratitude to your *wife* with jewelry. Do you mind if I show mine by selling it?"

He blinked in surprise, expected anger, but had to laugh again. "Are you always so delightfully honest?"

"Aye," she said without hesitation, and he laughed harder.

Kennedy was forced to release her or laugh in her face. Perhaps the laughter was a delayed response of hysteria. Or perhaps she was simply funny.

How was he supposed to make love to a woman who kept him laughing? There was only one answer. He stepped, closer yanked her against him, and kissed her. She gave a squeak of surprise. He thought for an instant he would laugh again, then she melted against him and the laughter vanished. She grasped his shoulders as she had when he kissed her at the ceremony, but this time, the heat of her fingers penetrated the thin fabric of his silk robe. When she squeezed the hard muscle, he wondered what her fingers would feel like around his hard length.

He flicked his tongue against her lips. She hesitated, then opened for him. Kennedy slipped his tongue inside her mouth and her tongue cautiously touched his. A jolt of desire tightened his bollocks. The woman could easily bring a man to his knees. A thought struck. She said that her desperation to marry stemmed from a need to care for her family, but what if it was something more? What if she was carrying another man's child?"

He wanted to laugh again, only this time the humor was dark. It would serve his father right for Kennedy's heir to be another man's offspring. Kennedy, however, wasn't so certain he liked the idea. He brushed off the thought. If she was already pregnant, that only meant Rose would return home soon.

Kennedy slid his hand down her back and over the curve of her firm buttocks. She drew a sharp breath as he gently undulated his erection against her belly. He broke the kiss and slid his mouth along her cheek to her ear. When he took her lobe into his mouth and nibbled, she wiggled in his grasp, and he realized he wanted her—badly.

He swept her into his arms and crossed to the bed. When he laid her on the mattress, her hair fanned around her face just as he'd imagined that first night. She really was lovely. He couldn't blame her if she carried another man's child. Hadn't he told her that a woman had just as much right as a man to see to her pleasures? A woman in her position, however, might find it prudent to bear her husband an heir first. For all he knew, that had been her plan. Perhaps she'd been engaged, and the man jilted her. Whatever the case, he could have done far worse.

With a flourish, he yanked the tie free on his robe and sloughed it from his back, then came down on top of her. Her soft curves molded to his body as if made for him. He cupped her face between his hands and kissed her gently. Slowly, she slid her hands up his shoulders and wrapped her arms around his neck.

He broke the kiss and slid his mouth downward along her jaw, her neck, to the rise of her breasts and finally to the nipple that now pressed like a pebble against the fabric of her night shift. He took one bud in his mouth and suckled. She drew a sharp breath. Desire swept through him.

When was the last time a woman had excited him so quickly? Jacqueline? He thrust his cock against her abdomen. She fisted his hair. He gave a low laugh then switched to her other breast. There was something to be said about marrying a woman who knew what she wanted.

He really had to get that damned shift off her.

Kenney levered up on his arms and looked down at her. "What do you say, love? Are you ready to take off that shift?" Her cheeks colored and Kennedy laughed, then rolled onto the mattress beside her. He stuffed his hands beneath his head. "Go ahead, I will watch."

Her mouth fell open. "You want to watch while I undress?"

He shrugged. "Why not? I let you watch while I took off my robe."

Her blush deepened. "Aye, but you are-are, and I am—" She broke off.

"There is no need to be shy with me, love," he said. "I told you. I don't mind that you're a woman who has already sought her pleasures."

She blinked, then fury played across her features, and he realized his mistake. Kennedy set upright ad reached for her, but too late.

She scrambled off the bed and backed up two paces. "If you believe I am a loose woman, why did you marry me?" Before he could answer, she said. "Oh, yes, of course. I forgot. Your father commanded you to marry, and that is all that matters."

An answering fury whipped through him and Kennedy shoved from the bed to his feet. Her wide-eyed gaze flicked to his erection, which jutted upward like a steel rod.

"Aye, madam, producing an heir is *all* that matters. Just as you needing money is all that matters to you."

"Thank heavens for that," she retorted. "Otherwise, I would be disappointed."

"Then you *are* one of those women who expect love," he said.

"Ha!" She burst out. "Thankfully, I do not suffer that malady."

An odd pain stabbed at his heart. "Then you won't mind if I carry on as I always have."

"As will I." She arched a brow. "You did say that you admired a woman who knew what she wanted and wasn't afraid to pursue it."

"You will not pursue your pleasure until I have an heir."

"That is not a point stipulated in the marriage contract."

He knew she was angry, knew the argument had gotten out of hand, but he couldn't stop himself from saying. "Test me on this, my dear, and you will find your lovers meeting me at a dawn appointment." With that, he quit the room.

ANNE GAVE THANKS WHEN SHE ENTERED THE BREAKFAST ROOM the following morning to find Kennedy absent. Her mother and sister were having coffee, and she slipped into the chair opposite her mother.

"Good morning, Mama. Louisa. How did you sleep?"

"Very well," her mother replied.

Anne kept her eyes on her cup as she poured coffee.

"I slept with Mama," Louisa said. "This house has noises that ours doesn't."

Anne smiled. "I think it's more accurate to say that Dover Hall has noises, while his lordship's townhouse is too quiet."

"His lordship?" her mother said.

Anne sighed inwardly. Leave it to her mother to notice the smallest slip. "It will take some time for me to grow accustomed to calling him by his Christian name," Anne said.

"Hmm," her mother intoned as she raised her cup.

Anne took a hearty drink of her coffee and didn't respond to her mother.

"We have decided to stay for two more days," her mother said.

Anne looked up. "Why?"

"It sounds as if you are disappointed we are staying," Louisa said.

Anne shook her head. "Not at all. I was just surprised, is all." She wasn't certain if that was the truth, however. She felt oddly self-conscious with her mother and sister here.

"We received a personal invitation from Kennedy's father to attend the ball tonight," her mother said.

"That was very kind of him," Anne replied, but she wondered if her husband would feel the same.

"I have only the one dress I brought with me," Louisa said.

Anne heard the hope in her sister's voice. At fourteen, Louisa wouldn't typically attend parties. But this party was held in honor of her sister's wedding. Of course, she would accompany them. Her presence would be a good excuse for Anne to leave early.

"There is no time to have anything sewn," Anne said.

Louisa nodded, but the enthusiasm in her eyes dimmed, and guilt stabbed when Louisa said, "Of course. The dress I have will do quite well."

Here she was newly married to a wealthy viscount and worried about spending money on dresses for her sister. Dared she spend his money?

Anne rose and went to the door and pulled the bell pull. She sat back down, and a moment later the maid entered.

"What is your name?" Anne asked.

The girl glanced nervously around the room. "Emma, my lady," she said, and curtsied.

Anne smiled reassuringly. "Emma, can you please tell the housekeeper that I would like to see her?"

The girl's eyes widened and she bobbed a curtsy, and said, "Aye, my lady." She whirled and hurried from the room.

Anne's mother gave her a curious look, but said nothing. Anne filled her plate with eggs and ham and began to eat.

A few minutes later, a short, thin woman of about fifty-five years entered. "You asked to see me, my lady?"

Anne smiled. "May I ask your name, ma'am?"

The woman looked startled, but said, "Mrs. Hampshire."

"It is a pleasure to meet you, Mrs. Hampshire. This is my mother, Lady Kinsley, and my sister, Lady Louisa."

Mrs. Hampshire curtsied, then looked at Anne expectantly.

"Mrs. Hampshire, do ye by chance know a dress shop where my sister can purchase a dress for the ball we are to attend tonight?"

"Why, yes, my lady, I know of several very nice dress shops downtown."

Anne beamed. "When you have a moment, if you could please write down the addresses, I would appreciate that."

Of course, my lady. Is there anything else?"

"Aye, now that you mention it. Can you tell me what would be the best time to go to one of the dress shops?"

"Not before one o'clock, my lady. You might begin at Mrs. Gerard's shop. She is known for opening earlier than many of the other shops and I have heard ladies say that they like her work."

"That is perfect, thank you very much, Mrs. Hampshire," Anne said. "Who do I speak to about having the carriage ready at one o'clock?"

"That would be the butler, Mr. Bingham," she said. "I can direct him to have the carriage ready for ye, ma'am."

"Thank you very much, Mrs. Hampshire."

The housekeeper curtsied, and Anne said, "Mrs. Hampshire, there is no need to be so formal. You will wear yourself out."

Mrs. Hampshire smiled. "Thank you, my lady. If there is nothing else..."

"You have been most helpful, thank you. That will be all," Anne said.

The housekeeper left, and Anne looked at Louisa. "Do you think you can be ready at one o'clock to go shopping?"

Louisa jumped up from her seat, raced around the table, and threw herself into Anne's arms.

Tears pricked her eyes.

*This is why I married a stranger.*

# CHAPTER 5

KENNEDY STOPPED AT THE OFFICE DOOR AND KNOCKED.

"Enter," the man inside called.

Kennedy open the door and entered. A large man who sat behind the desk looked up and smiled. "You're early." He rose and shook Kennedy's hand when he reached the desk.

"This is important, John."

John nodded toward the chair opposite his desk. Kennedy sat down while John resumed his seat.

"It's been nine days, Kennedy. A lifetime for you, I know. But a mere pittance for me."

Kennedy's chest constricted. "No clues as to her whereabouts, then, I take it?"

John's brows rose. "I didnae say that."

Kennedy sat forward in his chair. "You have something?"

John rested his arms on his desk and clasped his hands. "Your sister and her maid, Sarah, left your father's estate at eight p.m., the evening before you contacted me."

"What? You mean my father had only just sent her away? Had I been home instead of out at a damned ball, I would've gone to see him much earlier and perhaps—"

"Perhaps nothing," John cut in. "Whether an hour or day, unless your carriage crossed hers on the street, you simply couldn't have known."

John was right, of course. But it was still too bitter a pill to swallow. She'd been gone no more than an hour when Jacqueline came to his home. He refocused on John. "Is there anything else, anything at all? How did you discover this?"

John leaned back in his chair and flashed a wide smile. "No matter how hard you nobles try, you can never really hide anything from servants. Have you ever considered the possibility that by making your servants invisible to the world, you yourself stop seeing them?"

"Enough of the philosophical rantings," Kennedy said. "You are well aware that I don't hold with treating my servants as if they aren't human. So, you questioned the servants. What else did you learn?"

"It looks as though your father was telling the truth when he said Rose is no longer in Scotland. She took three large trunks, the sorts of trunks that one might take on a ship."

"France," Kennedy whispered.

"Let's hope so. If it were the Colonies..." his voice trailed off.

Kennedy shook his head. "We know no one in America. Despite my father's bravado, he clings to life like a man hanging from a cliff by his fingernails. Somewhere in the recesses of his diseased mind, he believes he will cheat death for a time. If I do produce an heir in the next nine months, and Rose does not return home safely, he knows I will kill him."

"Have you friends, associations, of any sort in France?" John asked.

Kennedy nodded. "Aye, many, even some distant relatives. But he knows better than to send my sister to any of them. However, he would make certain there was someone nearby who could help with any problems. He would also want to know if any problems arose."

John gave a slow nod. "My thoughts exactly. Which is why I have a man watching Chesterfield at all times.

Kennedy left John with this office, certain he'd hired the right man to help find his sister. It was John's logic—along with the fact he had barred the door when Kennedy had decided to begin the search for Rose himself. John was one of the few men he knew big enough to stop him. He was also one of the few men Kennedy knew who made sense when he argued a case. He'd been right, of course. Kennedy's first order of business was marrying a woman and getting her with child. In all likelihood, once he succeeded, his father really would bring Rose home. Kennedy still wasn't certain he would bring her home before a child was born, despite Kennedy's demands. However, once Anne was pregnant, Kennedy could join the search for his sister.

KENNEDY RETURNED HOME THAT AFTERNOON TO FIND HIS WIFE, her mother and sister out. When he questioned the staff, he learned they had gone dress shopping. For a woman in such need of money, she certainly didn't mind spending it on frivolous things at the first opportunity.

He headed to his office and threw himself into work, hoping to forget his inability to help his sister. He hadn't even bedded his wife yet. He winced at memory of last night's argument. He'd been completely in the wrong. Once his anger abated, he recognized the wide-eyed shock on her face when she'd caught sight of his erection. That look belonged to a woman who'd never seen a man's arousal.

He hadn't meant to insult her, but he meant what he said. The antiquated idea that a man could seek pleasure whenever and wherever he chose, while a woman was obligated to remain chaste, was ridiculous. Jacqueline hadn't been a virgin, and he hadn't cared. But Anne wasn't Jacqueline. She clearly considered any attack on her chastity an attack on her honor.

A COMMOTION IN THE HALLWAY JARRED KENNEDY FROM HIS work on the labor contracts he reviewed. He glanced at the clock. Four P.M. He had been working for over two hours. The voices in the hallway grew louder, and he recognized Louisa's laugh. Warmth rippled through him. Rose had often complained that she wanted a little sister. Louisa may not be exactly what she had in mind, but the two girls would get along famously.

The voices grew closer and he braced himself when the door burst open and Louisa rushed in with a dress box under her arm. She spotted him and broke into a bright smile. Anne and her mother entered the room. Anne's cheeks were flushed and her eyes were bright with laughter. She was breathtaking.

Kennedy rose and walked around his desk toward them.

"Kennedy, I am so glad you are home," Louisa cried.

He laughed. "Then I am glad, as well."

"Kennedy," the viscountess said as she removed her gloves.

"My lady." He gave a slight bow, then addressed his wife, "Anne."

"Good afternoon, my lord," she replied.

He saw none of the anger from the night before and prayed that she'd forgiven him.

Louisa hurried to the divan near the window and dropped the box she carried onto the cushion. "You must see this dress I have just purchased for the ball tonight."

Kennedy halted next to Anne. "The ball tonight?"

"Aye," Louisa said. "Mama has agreed to allow me to come." She tore the top off the box, but Kennedy was no longer looking at her.

"We are no' attending the ball tonight," he told Anne.

She frowned. "But your father and stepmother are hosting the party in honor of our marriage. We must attend."

He gave a harsh laugh. "Nae, we do not have to attend."

"We are not attending the ball?" Louisa asked.

Kennedy glanced at her. She stood, holding a pink velvet evening gown up against her body.

"My lord," Anne said, "is it not better to stay on good terms with your father?"

He snapped his gaze onto her. "I am on as good terms with him as is possible," he said in a level voice.

"Oh dear," Louisa said. "You are angry that we charged my dress and shoes to you, aren't you?"

He looked at the girl in surprise. "You charged the dress to me?" The moment the words left his mouth, he realized his mistake.

Tears appeared in the girl's eyes and she plopped down on the divan. The viscountess hurried to her daughter and sat beside her.

"Ye need not worry, my lord, I will pay for the dress," Anne said in a tight voice. She started toward her sister.

Kennedy grasped her arm. "Wait."

He released her and took the three steps to the couch and squatted eye level with Louisa. She wasn't crying—yet—but the sadness in her eyes tore at his heart. He placed a finger beneath her chin and gently tilted her head upward so that she has forced to meet his gaze.

"I don't at all mind paying for your dress," he said. "I simply hadn't planned on going to the party, so you caught me off guard." He smiled. "You know that ladies oftentimes catch gentlemen off guard."

Her expression cleared. "I have noticed that. I have a friend Robert. We've known each other since we were four. Of late, however, he sometimes says the strangest things. It's very silly and I've asked him if he has some sort of brain disease. That only seemed to upset him, though, and he gets tongue-tied. Is that what you mean?"

He laughed. "Well, I suspect that Robert's malady has more to do with the fact that you are a very pretty young lady, rather than a brother who wasn't planning to go to a party. But you have the general idea."

"If you do not want to go to the party tonight, that is quite all right. I do not mind returning the dress and the shoes and…" she gave him a sheepish smile, "the gloves."

He stood. "Not at all. Anne is correct. We should stay on good terms with my father. We shall all go."

Louisa leapt to her feet and threw her arms around him. "I wasn't at all happy about Anne marrying some stranger. But now I'm very glad she married you."

Kennedy felt his wife's eyes bore into the back of his head. He wasn't at all sure she was happy she had married him.

ANNE ENTERED THE BALLROOM OF HER FATHER-IN-LAW'S mansion on Kennedy's arm and took a deep breath as they paused in the doorway. Her mother and sister halted beside them. Dancers slid across the dancefloor in a rousing country dance and guests filled the rest of the space in the massive room.

"Oh my," Louisa breathed. "I have never seen a ballroom this large."

"Remember, you are to remain with me or Anne," their mother said.

"What of Kennedy?" Louisa smiled at him. "Surely, it is safe for me to stay with him if you and Anne are busy."

"I am sure Kennedy will be very busy," she replied.

He smiled down at her. "Louisa is welcome to remain with me, if she likes."

Louisa smiled back, adoration beaming in her eyes, and Anne realized Louisa had taken her words to heart and had embraced Kennedy as her new brother. Her heart tugged. It hadn't occurred to her that Louisa might benefit from the addition of a man into their family.

Their mother angled her head toward Kennedy. "As you wish, Kennedy." Uncharacteristic amusement shown in her eyes. "You may regret that invitation."

"There are so many people. Where do we begin?" Louisa asked.

"If ye like, I can introduce you to some ladies who might share some of your interests," Kennedy said.

Anne wondered how he might know what their interests were, but she nodded and thanked him.

The next hour was spent with Kennedy making introductions. Her head buzzed with names and music and the din of voices, but Anne had to admit that a couple of the ladies did appear quite interesting. Lady Hanna knew a great deal about agriculture, and the next lady they met, Miss Watson, clearly had a head for astronomy.

"I am surprised you associate with bluestockings," Anne said, when Miss Watson was whisked to the dance floor by a handsome gentleman.

Kennedy met her gaze. "I believe I told you that I respect a woman who knows what she wants and isn't afraid to pursue it." He lifted a brow. "Did you think I was lying?"

She narrowed her eyes. "I thought you were pursuing something that you wanted at that moment."

He laughed, then introduced them to two more ladies who talked of nothing but sewing, parties and dresses.

"Is that more to your liking, my lady? he asked when they finally left the ladies.

"It wasn't to my liking," Louisa said. "Forgive me for saying so, Kennedy, but they were excessively dull."

"Louisa," their mother hissed in a low voice when two ladies glanced their way.

"Don't reprimand her for speaking the truth," Kennedy said. "I happen to agree." He looked at Louisa. "Still, I am surprised. I know you like dresses and parties, so why did you find them dull?"

"Of course, I like dresses and parties," she said as if talking to a child. "They are great fun. But I wouldn't go on about them and talk of nothing else. Have they no other interests?"

Kennedy chuckled. "Not that I know of."

Louisa made a face. "Must we be friends with them?"

"For heaven's sake, Louisa," her mother said. "Keep your voice down."

Louisa hung her head. "Of course, Mama."

Kennedy leaned close to Louisa and whispered, "Never fear, you need not be friends with anyone you don't like."

She beamed. "Thank you. I'm thirsty, Mama. May I have champagne?"

"You may not," she replied. "You may have lemonade."

Louisa slanted a look up at Kennedy. "Kennedy, don't you think that fourteen is old enough to have just a little champagne?"

Their mother stiffened.

He tweaked one of Louisa's curls. "I think that fourteen is old enough to know better than to ask her brother to countermand her mother's instructions."

Louisa blinked and Anne thought she would pout. Instead, she shrugged and said, "I suppose I have much to learn about having a brother."

He laughed again and Anne noted a tinge of sadness this time.

The orchestra struck up a waltz.

"You and Anne haven't dance," Louisa said. "The waltz is so romantic. You must dance."

Kennedy looked at her. "Shall we, my lady?"

The last thing she wanted was to dance with him, but how could she refuse? She nodded, and he grasped her hand, tucked it into the crook of his arm, and led her toward the dance floor.

Once they were out of earshot of her mother and sister, she said, "You need not dance with me."

He looked at her. "There is nothing strange in a man dancing with his wife."

She wasn't his wife—not truly. Not yet.

"True, but Louisa forced you to ask me."

"Never fear, few people can force me to do anything."

They reached the dance floor. He pulled her close and stepped into the music. She wasn't surprised to find he was an excellent dancer.

"Who are the few people who can force you to do anything?" she asked.

His gaze snapped onto her. "What?"

"You said few people can force you to do anything. Who are those few people?"

"I suppose there is only one person in truth," he said, as if speaking to himself.

"Who?"

He seemed lost in thought, and only shook his head. "It is of no consequence."

"Your father?" she asked.

His full mouth thinned and he looked at her. "Why ask questions you already know the answers to?"

She considered. "I am sorry you were forced to marry me."

He released a breath and guided them past a couple, then sidestepped another couple who nearly rammed them.

"It isn't your fault, Anne."

"True," she replied. "But you're clearly unhappy with marriage."

Interest lit his eyes. "Are you saying that because we didn't consummate our marriage last night?"

Embarrassment warmed her cheeks. "I-I didn't mean that, at all."

The interest turned to amusement. "We are not the first married couple not to consummate their marriage on their wedding night."

Anne nibbled on her lip. "There is always tonight."

"Have you plans for me, my sweet?"

What plans did she have? "We are not truly married until…"

His amusement vanished. "You want to earn that five thousand pounds as quickly as possible. I am a fool."

Anne gasped. Then anger whipped through her. "Why not? This is a business arrangement after all—nothing more."

His eyes darkened. "Then I shall be at your service tonight, madam."

"If you are certain that you are up to it, my lord? I don't want to inconvenience you."

"Too late," he shot back. "You have inconvenienced me a great deal."

He yanked her against him and turned her in a tight whirl that made her dizzy—and aware of his hard length.

"I must now devise a way not to embarrass myself in front of Edinburgh's elite," he said.

Then she found herself being whirled off the dance floor and out the balcony doors.

KENNEDY BROUGHT ANNE TO A HALT. SHE TRIED TO SHOVE AWAY from him, but he tightened his grip and kissed her. Then released her. She took two faltering steps backward.

"Just a preview of things to come," he said.

"How very fortunate for me," she said.

"Oh, it will be, that I promise."

She released a frustrated breath, then turned and hurried back into the ballroom.

Kennedy started after her, then thought better of it and pivoted, headed for the gardens. He crossed the balcony, took the three steps down to the lawn, and slowed to a stroll. Anne didn't deserve his disdain. She was right. Their marriage was a business arrangement. Oddly, the thought bothered him. She was also correct in that he wasn't happy being married. He'd known he would someday marry, but it galled him that his father had forced the issue and had even chosen his bride.

Underneath it all, though, he feared for Rose. He couldn't allow himself to dwell on her. For the moment, he felt certain she was safe. The longer she was away, however, the greater the chances that her keepers would grow careless. And he couldn't consider what would happen if his father died.

He needed Anne to bear him a son just as much as she wanted to. He couldn't fault her for that. Tonight, he would consummate their marriage. A small sense of satisfaction arose. If his father had any idea that he hadn't consummated the marriage last night, he'd be furious. Now that he thought of it, he should have married long ago and simply never consummated the marriage. That would've driven his father mad, and he would have had no recourse to kidnap Rose. He was wrong. His father would have secreted her away and demanded Kennedy bed is wife and bear a child.

Why hadn't it occurred to him that his father would use Rose? Because, despite everything, Kennedy simply had never believed his father would put his own daughter in jeopardy. He wouldn't underestimate the old man again.

"Kennedy."

Kennedy halted. Bloody hell. He turned to face Jacqueline. "What are you doing here?"

"I saw you and Anne leave the ballroom, but she returned immediately. Is something amiss?"

"What is amiss, Jacqueline, is that my father has kidnapped my sister and blackmailed me into marriage."

She stepped closer and laid a hand on his arm. "You know your father will never allow any harm to come to Rose."

"He threatened to marry her to Granbury. There is no worse harm that can come to her."

She shook her head. "I don't believe he would do it."

"Then you are a fool."

She stepped closer. "Does she please you?"

He didn't have to ask who the 'she' was. "Very much so," he said.

"Does she please you as much as I used to?"

Kennedy stared down at her. Even in the pale moonlight she was beautiful. "Aye, she pleases me very much."

Jacqueline laid her palms on his chest. "Perhaps you have forgotten how much I please you."

He grasped her hands and removed them from his chest. "You should remember that you're married to my father."

"You know how ill he is, Kennedy. He hasn't been able to..." She looked up at him through her lashes. "I am very lonely."

He gave her a cold smile. "Perhaps there is a stable hand who will oblige. I understand you like stable hands."

"You know that is a vicious lie."

"I know nothing of the sort. In fact, I would be surprised if it wasn't true."

She slapped him. His cheek stung. He wanted to shake her, demand to know why she'd chosen his father. But he knew why.

She whirled toward the mansion and hurried away. He watched until she disappeared from view. Had she always been so cold and calculating? He thought back. She was driven. That was something he'd always admired about her. What he hadn't understood was the motivation behind that drive. She would have what she wanted at all costs. Were all women like that?

He thought of Anne. Aye, she was determined, as well. Unlike Jacqueline, however, she never pretended to love him. Of course, he'd known her for less than two days. There was still time for her to pretend many things. He recalled her ire moments ago, and wondered if she were capable of doing anything but showing what was in her heart. He sighed. Time would tell.

# CHAPTER 6

ANNE REENTERED THE BALLROOM AND SCANNED THE ROOM FOR her mother and Louisa, but found no sign of them. She stopped a passing waiter and took a glass of champagne from his tray, then glanced back in the direction of the open balcony doors. The man really was impossible. She took two deep gulps of champagne. He had better get her with child soon, because she was liable to murder him. Her stomach performed a somersault at the memory of his promise, *"I will be at your service tonight, madam."*

The words were spoken in anger, but she hadn't missed the deep timbre of his voice and the intensity of his gaze when he'd said them. Anne took another gulp of champagne. She'd never known a more insufferable man. Perhaps she should ask her mother how to deal with him. Nae. Her mother would be aghast to learn they hadn't consummated their marriage. A lady always submitted to her husband's commands in the bedchambers.

Anne lifted the champagne glass to her lips and found only a small mouthful remained. Where was another waiter? She scanned the room and caught sight of Jacqueline entering the ballroom from the balcony. Anne hadn't seen her outside. Had she spoken with Kennedy?

Had Kennedy returned to the ballroom? She searched the room again, but there were so many people, she might have overlooked him. Jacqueline turned, and their eyes met. Anne read something there. Guilt? Jacqueline started toward her. Oh Lord, she was in no mood to speak to the woman. She didn't like her. But she couldn't ignore her. Jacqueline knew that she had seen her.

"There she is, Mama," Louisa said behind her.

Anne turned as her mother and sister neared her. "I'm so relieved to see you," she blurted.

Her mother's eyes sharpened and Anne realized her mistake. She thought her mother would say something, but her eyes shifted past Anne and Jacqueline appeared beside them an instant later.

"Good evening, Lady Kinsley," she said. "Lady Louisa, you look lovely."

"Thank you," Louisa bubbled over. "This is a special dress I wore just for this party."

"It's absolutely perfect," Jacqueline said, then she turned to Anne. "I am so glad to find you. I have been looking for you for the last hour." Anne had the feeling she was lying. "The earl would like to meet you," Jacqueline said.

The earl wanted to meet her? She recalled Kennedy saying that she wouldn't meet his father if he had his way. She glanced toward the balcony doors, but saw no sign of him.

"I hope he hasn't fallen asleep," Jacqueline said. "He now sleeps far more than he is awake." She smiled at Anne's mother. "It is so difficult." She sighed, then looked at Anne. "Come, let's go up to his chambers."

"Perhaps I should wait for Kennedy," Anne said.

"Do you know where he is?" Jacqueline asked.

"I left them out on the balcony," Anne replied.

"I just came from the gardens," Jacqueline said. "He was taking a walk."

Shock reverberated through Anne. "You saw him in the gardens?"

"Oh, yes, walking in the gardens is a favorite activity of ours."

Anne caught the startled look on her mother's face.

"Kennedy has been so wonderful during his father's illness," Jacqueline said. "I don't know what I would have done without him."

Her tone was intimate. But why wouldn't it be? They were family. Anne was being ridiculous. But it had been disturbing the way Jacqueline rested her hand on Kennedy's arm yesterday morning at the wedding feast. Anne was no fool. She'd watched her friends flirt and bat their eyes to gain a young man's attention. A woman didn't touch a man's arm like that unless they were close.

Jacqueline smiled sweetly. "Please, Joseph has expressly asked to see you." She angled her head toward Anne's mother." You will excuse us, Lady Kinsley. Come along, Anne."

Anne hesitated, then nodded. "I will return soon, Mama. Please let Kennedy know where I am. I am sure he will return from his walk in the garden soon."

Her mother nodded, then Anne followed Jacqueline through the crowd to a hallway, but she wished mightily she was in the gardens with her husband.

KENNEDY REENTERED THE BALLROOM WITH THE INTENTION OF finding Anne and Louisa and returning home. They had stayed long enough for Louisa to have gotten her fill of the party. He caught sight of them near the left hand wall and started toward them. He brushed past a group of men, and waited for three ladies to pass when he heard his name called. Kennedy cursed, and turned to face his uncle as the older man reached him.

"Can we speak?" Ranald asked.

"Can it wait?" Kennedy asked. "I am meeting my wife's mother and sister."

Ranald's expression brightened. "I had hoped to meet your wife."

"Come along, then." Kennedy turned and dodged two passing gentlemen, then pushed through the throng that seemed to have grown during his walk in the garden.

They reached the two women, and the viscountess said, "Kennedy I am relieved to see you," then broke off when Ranald stepped up beside him.

"My lady, this is my uncle, Lord Ranald," Kennedy said. "Ranald, Lady Kinsley and her daughter Lady Louisa."

"Ma'am." Ranald bowed over the older woman's hand. Louisa curtsied and he bowed in return.

"What is amiss?" Kennedy demanded, then realized he had spoken too loudly when a group of nearby man looked their way. "What has happened? he said in a low voice.

She hesitated, and Kennedy said, "You may speak freely in front of my uncle."

She glanced at the older man, then said in a low voice, "Your stepmother took Anne up to meet your father."

"Bloody hell," he cursed. "I instructed her not to leave the ballroom," he said.

The dowager viscountess's brows rose. "You clearly do not know your wife, if you expected that command to be followed."

"My wife will learn to heed my commands," he said.

Amusement flickered in her eyes. "It may be you who learns a few lessons," she murmured.

"I take it you believe a wife has the right to ignore her husband's wishes?"

"Not at all. I am simply experienced enough to know that a

marriage—a happy marriage—is not built on obedience to commands."

"She has a point," Ranald said.

Kennedy gave his uncle a narrow-eyed look. "I can see an interesting road lies ahead for me."

"Of that you may be assured," the viscountess said. "First, however, you might want to rescue your stepmother from Anne."

He blinked. "I beg your pardon? It is Anne who will need rescuing."

She gave him a polite smile. "You have not yet had cause to learn this, but Anne has a temper."

He barked a laugh. "Indeed, I have learned that, madam." He excused himself and headed for his father's chambers to rescue someone, though he knew not who.

Anne's heart squeezed at sight of the elderly man who sat propped up in bed reading a book. He was more than just ill. The paleness of his skin and the tremble in his hands told her he was dying. Still, a keen intelligence stared back at her through the pale blue eyes that watched their approach.

Jacqueline hurried to his bed, then pressed a kiss to his cheek, and said, "My dear, this is Anne."

Anne stopped a few feet away.

"Come closer." He beckoned with a gnarled hand.

Anne did as instructed and stopped beside Jacqueline, then curtsied.

"You are very beautiful," he said.

"Thank you, my lord," Anne said.

"What do you think of my son? Will he give you a son?"

Anne started at the question. How did she know the answer to such a question?

"I am sure he will do his best, my lord."

The man's eyes sharpened. "*Will do his best?* By now, I expect you to have been working hard to produce an heir."

Anne blinked. She and Kennedy had been married but a day. How hard could they be 'working' to have a child? "Forgive me, sir, but it is not proper for a wife to speak of such things, especially to her husband's father."

"She is right, my dear," Jacqueline said. "Anne is a new bride."

"Bah! We have no time to stand on such ceremony." His gaze locked with hers. "I know you need the five thousand pounds I promised once you produce an heir. I will pay you an extra five thousand pounds if you remain in Kennedy's bed every night between now and when you get pregnant."

Anne stared. The man was mad. But it was more than that, she realized. Here was the reason Kennedy hadn't wanted her to meet his father. The man was trying to control his life right down to how many times they...

"Forgive me, my lord, but I cannot see how you could possibly confirm I was deserving of the extra five thousand pounds." She lifted her brows. "Unless, that is, you intend to be in the bed with us."

To her shock, the earl didn't so much as bad an eye at her sarcasm, but said, "If you get pregnant soon, then I will be satisfied that you lived up to your end of the bargain."

Kennedy might be insufferable, but this man was cruel. "There was always the chance that I might get pregnant the first or second night we are together," she said with sickeningly sweet sarcasm.

"Are you willing to take the risk that you will not receive the extra money if you don't get pregnant right away?" he countered.

"Ah, I see. If I don't get pregnant immediately, you will assume that Kennedy and I are not sharing a bed. What happens if we share a bed every night, and I do not get pregnant?"

"I am certain Kennedy is skilled enough to make his time in your bed worthwhile."

"My God, you have bollocks. Whether I get pregnant right away, a year from now, or five years from now, it will have nothing to do with you."

"But it has a great deal to do with Kennedy," he replied. "My son will see to it that you have a child within a year."

The conversation was insane. "Then why offer me more money?" she asked.

"I take no chances when it comes to the heir of my title."

"In case you have forgotten, you have an heir: my husband. And by-the-by it isn't just your title. There is mine, as well."

He nodded. "Aye, my grandson will be the eighth Earl of Buchanan, as well as Viscount Kinsley. That is why I chose you as Kennedy's bride."

She'd had enough. "Was there anything else you wanted, my lord, besides ensuring that my husband and I were spending enough time in bed together?"

He regarded her. "You will suit Kennedy well."

That, Anne hadn't expected.

"What has he told you about me?"

She hadn't expected that either. What was she supposed to say? She gave him a cool smile. "Nothing, really. I'm sure you understand we haven't spent our time talking."

Satisfaction lit his gaze. He nodded. "Good, very good. It hadn't occurred to me you might be beautiful, but the fact that you are will hold Kennedy's interest for a while."

*For a while?* Her heart felt as if it had been pierced with a knife.

"I expect you to name your son after me," he said.

"After you?" It wasn't uncommon for a father to name his son after his own father. Somehow, Anne doubted that

Kennedy would want to follow that tradition. "I will discuss it with Kennedy, of course."

He waved his hand dismissively, and she wanted to knock the gnarled thing aside. "He will do as you ask."

Then she understood. "If you suggest that we name our child after you, he will defy you," she said more to herself than him. "But you expect me to manipulate him for your own ends."

"It is my right," he said as if that was sufficient.

Anne laughed. "Not quite. What of my father? Perhaps I would like to name our child after him."

At last, she saw ire in his eyes. Satisfaction shot through her.

"I will give you another five thousand pounds, if you talk Kennedy into naming your son after me," he said.

She couldn't believe her ears. "Keep your five thousand pounds. Keep all your money." Anne whirled and stopped short at sight of Kennedy standing in the doorway.

# CHAPTER 7

KENNEDY COULDN'T TAKE HIS EYES OFF HIS WIFE AS HE ENTERED the room. She had just told his father to keep all his money. Kennedy reached her side, grasped her hand and brought it to his lips.

She frowned, her expression turning suspicious when he said, "I missed you, my dear." He released her and looked at his father. "I didn't realize you intended to meet Anne tonight, sir."

"If you had known, you wouldn't have brought her," his father replied.

Kennedy smiled coolly. "You have Anne's sister to thank for our being here. I hadn't planned on coming, but she had her heart set on attending the party and I couldn't disappoint her."

Frustration flickered across his father's face, and Kennedy cursed his own tongue. Normally, he would have pressed any advantage once he'd broken down his father's façade. But his father wasn't above changing the terms of an agreement if pushed hard enough, and Kennedy needed to assure that Rose returned home as soon as possible.

"I believe we have been here long enough to satisfy her," Anne said. "If you don't mind, I would like to go home."

Kennedy smiled at her. "Of course, my dear."

"It was a pleasure to meet you, my lord," Anne said. "I hope you feel better soon." She shifted her attention to Jacqueline and said in a cool tone, "My lady, thank you for a lovely party."

"Of course," Jaqueline said. "We are so very happy for you and Kennedy."

"Remember what I said," his father said to Anne.

She smiled. "Never fear, sir, I shall be giving everything you said a great deal of thought." Her gaze shifted onto Kennedy. "Shall we go?"

He angled his head in acknowledgement. "If you are ready, my dear." Without a backwards glance, they left.

To his wife's credit she remained quiet until they were halfway down the first flight of stairs. "Forgive me, sir, but I must tell you that your father is an abominable man."

Kennedy couldn't help himself. He laughed so hard his eyes watered.

They reached the next floor and she shot him a hard frown as they continued down the dim hallway. "I fail to see the humor in the situation. He had the gall to offer me another five thousand pounds if I spend every night in your bed until I am certain I am pregnant."

Kennedy looked sharply at her. He hadn't heard that. "I will speak to him."

She threw up her hands. "Why bother? He is clearly insane —and there is no talking to an insane person." Her expression turned sheepish. "I do not think he likes me very much."

They turned a corner in the hallway.

"He doesn't like anyone very much," Kennedy said.

"I can well believe that, but most people aren't his daughter-in-law."

"That does go too far, even for him," Kennedy said. "How does he think he will verify that you have kept your end of the bargain?"

They reached another set of stairs and he gestured for her to precede him.

"I asked that very thing," she said. "The only way he could be certain is if he were in the room with us."

Kennedy blinked. "Never say you said that to him."

"Of course, I did."

They reached the next level and sounds of the orchestra wafted up to them.

"He had the temerity to say that as long as I got pregnant right away, he would take my word that I had kept up my end of the bargain," she went on. "It would serve him right, if I didn't get pregnant anytime soon."

Alarm shot through him. "Did you tell him we hadn't consummated the marriage?"

A blush crept up her cheeks. "Nae. It is none of his business. About that, sir—"

"My fault altogether," he cut in.

She looked up at him in surprise, then smiled. His heart jumped.

"Thank you," she said.

How different she was from Jacqueline. They seldom fought —well, they seldom fought when they were lovers. But on the rare occasion they did, she made him feel as if her acceptance of his apology was a boon from on high.

Kennedy gave Anne a sideways glance. "Are you against having a child immediately?"

She shook her head. "Of course not. I expected to have children once I married." She looked up at him, a wry grin on her face. "I told him he could keep all his money. So, it seems I've talked myself out of the five thousand pounds he was going to give me once we have a son."

He'd heard that. Had she known he'd been outside the room? Her responses to his father had been so different than Jacqueline's. So…unaffected.

"Never mind," he said. "What matters is in the contract. I will ensure that he pays you the money."

She released a sigh. "The birth of our child is reduced to a business transaction. I am not certain I like that."

"Isn't that why you married me, for money?" His heart unexpectedly accelerated.

She slowed as they turned another corner and the music from the orchestra grew louder. "It's a common enough reason to marry," she said. "But I'm liking less and less the idea of taking money for bearing a child, whether it is a day from now, a year from now or five years from now."

"If it is a day from now, I will consider that most miraculous," he said with a grin.

She laughed, and he found he liked the sound. "I promise you, that will not happen," she said. "Still, I think I will refuse the money."

"You could always put it into a trust for our son." Our son. His chest tightened at the vision of her cradling their son before the hearth in their private chambers.

"I will have to think of another way to pay for the upkeep at Dover Hall." She looked up at him, again, with mischief in her eyes. "You may begin giving me expensive pieces of jewelry anytime you like."

Again, he laughed so hard his eyes watered.

HALFWAY HOME, A LARGE CRACK SOUNDED OUTSIDE THE carriage. Kennedy yanked Anne to him as the coach listed hard to the right. He slammed into the carriage wall. The ladies screamed. Louisa crashed into him. He hugged both women close as the carriage came to a jolting halt. The interior lamp went out and they were plunged into darkness.

"Mamma," Louisa cried, and clung to Kennedy.

"It's all right, Louisa," he murmured, then said, "Lady Kinsley, are you unharmed?"

"Aye. Louisa—" she began.

"I have her," Kennedy said. "She is unharmed. Anne, as well."

The carriage rocked, then the door to Kennedy's right was wrenched open and moonlight illuminated the interior of the carriage.

The driver stuck his head inside the carriage. "Is anyone hurt?" he demanded.

Kenney spotted Anne's mother, leaning against the carriage wall on the other side of the door. "The viscountess, James."

The footman helped her from the coach. Kennedy handed out Louisa, then Anne, and leapt from the carriage onto the sidewalk of the quiet street.

The right rear wheel broke, my lord."

"So I gathered," Kennedy said. "My lady." He took a step to the viscountess. The sleeve of her left shoulder was torn and a gash in her arm oozed blood. Kennedy gently turned her toward the streetlight and examined her. "You must have fallen against the lamp."

She nodded. "It is nothing."

"We will have a doctor attend to the wound once we reach home."

A carriage turned onto the street and slowed as they neared, then stopped. The door opened, and Kennedy's uncle stepped to the ground.

He strode to where they stood. "Is everyone unharmed?"

Kennedy nodded. "Fortunately, we weren't going fast."

"Let me take you home," Ranald said.

"Thank you." Kennedy turned to the driver. "James, I will send Matthew back with a new wheel. You and Michael remain here until they arrive."

James nodded. "Aye, my lord."

Kennedy got the ladies into the carriage, then he and Ranald stepped inside and they started away.

At home, they gathered in the drawing room while Ranald sent his carriage for the doctor. Kennedy roused Matthew and instructed him to take men to deliver the wheel and repair the carriage.

The doctor arrived half an hour later. Despite Lady Kinsley's insistence that she was fine, the doctor insisted on six stitches, then sent her to bed with a small dose of laudanum. The doctor left, and Anne sent Kennedy a grateful look, then went upstairs with her mother and sister.

"Would you like a drink?" Kennedy asked Ranald when the ladies had gone.

"Scotch, if you please," he said. "I'm glad for this opportunity to speak with you, Kennedy. Congratulations on your marriage, by-the-by. I'm sorry I missed the ceremony. I had no idea you were to marry."

Kennedy poured two scotches, then turned and motioned to the two hearth chairs. His uncle took the chair to the left. Kennedy handed him a glass of scotch and sat in the chair to the right.

"We had a very small ceremony by special license," Kennedy said.

Ranald nodded. "So I gathered. I feel certain your father had something to do with the marriage. I saw him the day before yesterday. He isn't looking well."

Kennedy took a hefty drink of scotch. He shook his head. "Nae, he isn't at all looking well."

Ranald regarded him. "I should think that you would be rejoicing."

"I will not be sorry when he is gone," Kennedy said.

"What the devil is going on?" his uncle demanded.

Kennedy took another drink of his whisky. "What do you mean?"

"There's too many strange things afoot. Pray, do not tell me you suddenly fell in love. Marriage was not on your agenda. And where is Rose? I didn't see her at Chesterfield when I visited your father. When I inquired, he said she was away. What does that mean?"

Ranald was as different from his brother as Kennedy was from his father. Kennedy had always liked his uncle, who was far too intelligent for his own good. "The earl sent her away and won't tell me where," Kennedy said. "He forced my marriage to Anne by threatening to marry Rose to Granbury if I didn't comply."

"By God, that goes too far, even for him," Ranald growled.

Kennedy nodded. "We both have underestimated my father for a long time."

Ranald nodded slowly. "Now that you're married, will Rose return home?"

Kennedy gave a harsh laugh. "Nae, there is more to the blackmail. I must produce an heir in the next year."

A rare flush of anger darkened Ranald's normally tranquil eyes. "By God, what is wrong with the man?"

"He is dying," Kennedy said with more calm than he felt. "This is a desperate attempt at eternal life."

"We all die," the older man said with heat. "A moment ago, I would've said, in his own way, he loves Rose. Now, I'm no' sure if even that is true. How long has she been gone?"

"Seven days."

"It's unlikely she'll come to any harm." His mouth thinned. "As long as he doesn't die. Have ye any idea where she is?"

"The earl said she wasn't in Scotland. Based on information I received from his servants, I'm inclined to think that's true."

Ranald nodded slowly. "France."

Kennedy nodded. "France is a big country, however. I could search Paris for years and never find her."

"Surely you plan to try?"

Kennedy grunted. "I have already begun. The only thing stopping me from going myself is the fact that I must immediately sire an heir."

Ranald frowned. "Does Joseph intend to keep Rose hidden until your first child is born?"

"Kennedy nodded. "That is exactly what he intends. I demanded that he bring Rose home once it is confirmed that my wife is pregnant. In truth, he could just as easily not comply."

Ranald leaned forward, elbows resting on his knees. "Tell me how I can help."

# CHAPTER 8

THE FOLLOWING MORNING, ANNE FOUND HER WAY INTO THE conservatory. The building was set off from the house in a secluded corner of the gardens. The paned glass structure rested on a foundation of waist-high stones. She entered the building and knew she was home. A light rain began to patter on the glass. Anne looked up at the gray clouds that inched across the sky. Even on an overcast day like today, she could remain here for hours. She strolled through the aisles, marveling at the variety of flowers, ferns and dwarfed trees. She found roses, thistle, and even heather. Anne paused to brush her finger against the petals of a lavender sweet pea and caught sight of a chaise lounge, table and chairs in the far corner. This was even better than she'd expected.

She stepped around a fig tree, then an apricot and plum, and continued to the chaise. A modest hearth was located nearby. Too bad she hadn't brought a book. Rain pattered a little harder on the glass. She looked up at the sky. The clouds had darkened. Next time she would bring a book. For now, she would start a fire and spend a little time with her thoughts.

With a sigh, Anne knelt at the hearth. She got a low fire

burning, then sat on the chaise and stared up at the black clouds. What kind of family had she married into? The earl was clearly a bitter and power-hungry man. His wife. Anne shuddered. Lady Buchanen was far too familiar with her stepson. Were she and Kennedy having an affair? Kennedy seemed to want to avoid her, and Anne had detected no affinity on his part for her. Had she made advances toward him? Anne could well believe it.

Kennedy didn't fit with them. Yesterday, when he told Louisa that he didn't mind buying dresses for her, and that he would gladly take them to the ball, he'd spoken like a real brother. The way he had hugged Anne to him and grabbed Louisa when the carriage wheel broke had caught her off guard. He was a man of action, and he cared about them—in some way, at any rate.

She wasn't certain what to make of the fact that he hadn't come to her room last night. True, the night had been more eventful than expected. Still, shouldn't a husband want to bed his wife? Despite his father's demands that they have a child immediately, perhaps Kennedy didn't want her. She recalled their wedding night. He had seemed… enthusiastic, until, that is, she'd learned he thought she was loose. Would the man never get it through his head that she cared about her honor? Whatever the case, she had to demand her wifely rights. It simply wasn't right that a marriage wasn't consummated. Her mother would be aghast if she learned they were not yet truly married.

She started from her thoughts at a sudden gust of air that swept through the conservatory. She straightened and realized the door had been opened. The door slammed closed and she jumped to her feet. An instant later, she glimpsed Kennedy amongst the foliage. He neared and his gaze met hers. He wore a dark coat with no tie and his collar lay open, revealing tanned flesh.

He neared her and said, "What the devil are you doing out here?" Then he saw the fire and nodded. "I can see this is already a favorite spot of yours."

Anne smiled. "Even on a day like today, it's a very pleasant room to be in."

He took off his dripping coat and shook the water from it. "My mother used to spend a lot of time here." He hung the coat over the back of a chair. "It's raining hard. I imagine we can wait just a little while to see if the rain will let up before returning to the house."

A tremor rippled through her. Stuck alone with him in a room with nowhere to go?

"If you have work to do, you needn't worry about keeping me company," she said. "I don't mind being alone."

He pinned her with his gaze. "Is my company so terrible that you can't bear to be alone with me for a short while?"

"Oh no, that is not at all what I meant." She blew out a frustrated breath. "I don't know what it is about you, but I always end up saying the wrong thing."

Amusement glittered in his eyes. "You wouldn't, per chance, be speaking of a similar effect to that which Louisa mentioned yesterday about her friend Robert always saying the wrong thing about her?"

She narrowed her eyes. "Hardly. That would imply some sort of affection, and I know how much you abhor such feelings from your wife."

To her surprise, he laughed. "You prove my point. You have some, if only a little, affection for me."

"Affection? How can I have affection for you? I hardly know you."

He grinned. "I'm a charming fellow."

Damn his soul, he was. But she wasn't about to admit that. "I feel certain you have charmed many a lady, my lord."

"The only lady I'm interested in charming is you."

She blinked. "I beg your pardon?"

"I believe you understand me," he said.

"Well, of course, I understand you. That is, I know what you said. As to your meaning, that could be anything."

"Come now, Anne, my meaning really can't be just *anything*."

The way he said 'anything' left little doubt as to what he meant. Heaven help her, it had gotten awfully warm in the room.

"They will probably begin to worry about us back at the house," she said. "Perhaps we should return."

He crossed to where she stood and stopped inches away. "I don't think they will worry about us overly much." He wrapped an arm around her waist and tugged her against him.

She immediately detected his hard length against her abdomen. "Oh dear," she breathed."

"Oh dear, indeed," he said, and covered her mouth with his.

Her knees weakened and she grasped his shoulders to keep herself upright. He laughed low and deep, then gently thrust his tongue between her lips and into her mouth. He tasted of scotch. His hold tightened around her waist, pulling her impossibly close. Her head swam. He broke the kiss and pressed warm kisses along her cheek to her neck. She shivered.

"Perhaps we should go to your bed chambers, my lord."

"We would never make it there without being waylaid by a family member," he murmured against her flesh, "and I have no desire to be interrupted."

She cried out when he swung her into his arms. He laid her on the chaise lounge and came down on top of her. For an instant, he felt too heavy, though she found she liked the feeling. Then he levered up on his elbows and kissed her neck. He tugged her sleeve down and kissed her shoulder. An intense ache thrummed between her legs in rhythm with her heartbeat.

She started at the realization that they were surrounded by glass.

"My lord, anyone can see inside the conservatory. Perhaps we really should return to the house."

"At the very least, while I am making love to you, you could try calling me by my Christian name," he said.

She blinked. Was he reprimanding her—now? "As you wish, *Kennedy*," she retorted.

He froze, then slowly lifted his head and met her gaze. "Have I peeved you again, my sweet?"

"You seem to make a habit of it," she said.

"This time, you may be as peeved with me as you like," he said. "But we shall consummate our marriage."

She should have been ashamed, but, in truth, that was exactly what she wanted.

Eyes locked with hers, he began inching up her skirt. She didn't flinch, didn't move. At last, his fingers made contact with her outer thigh. He flattened his palm against her flesh and slid his hand upward. His hand was so warm. No man had ever touched her so intimately. He slid off her onto the chaise beside her and continued his hand's upward climb. When he neared the apex between her legs, she tensed. He gently kissed her cheek then nibbled her ear. She twisted slightly at the tickle. Then realized his fingers were brushing the intimate curls. Gently, he slipped a finger between her moist folds. She jammed her eyes shut and gripped his arm.

"Relax, love," he said. "I won't hurt you."

She wasn't afraid of being hurt, it's just, she had never imagined a man would touch her there. However, to her surprise when his fingers brushed the sensitive nub, a tingle of pleasure rippled through her. She drew a breath. He began nibbling her ear again and the tingle traveled from her ear to the place where he brushed her sex. He applied a little more pressure and began massaging her.

"Good heavens," she breathed.

The ache intensified. He flicked his tongue against her ear. The sensation was almost sinful. She started when he slid a finger inside her.

"My goodness, Kennedy, do you think you should be doing that?"

He laughed. "That and much more, if you will allow me."

*Much more?* She couldn't imagine anything more--then he began to slide his finger in and out of her. A strange sense of pleasure rippled deep within her. He swirled his tongue. Heaven help her, how could something so innocent illicit such a decedent response?

"You set me on fire," he whispered, and her insides turned to jelly.

He quickened his movements inside her. She should be ashamed. But she liked the sensation, liked the slide of his warm digit in and out of her. Was she supposed to like this? Her mother had explained what took place between a man and a woman, but she hadn't told Anne about *this*, about the need that made her want to close her legs around Kennedy's hand and beg him to end the torture.

She became aware of his kisses moving down along her neck. His tongue flicked the sensitive flesh, then he gently sucked.

"Let go," he whispered. "Give in to the pleasure."

He nipped at her neck. A string of pleasure shot from her neck to the nub he massaged. She cried out with a pleasure that caused spots to race across her vision. Anne seized his arm and squeezed as the spasm rolled over her a second time.

Gently, he stroked her until the pleasure dissipated into a soft echo. She was still breathing hard as he unfastened the falls on his breeches. She didn't look down at his manhood—she'd seen that and didn't need to be reminded that it was much larger than his finger. When he levered over her, she knew a moment of panic. Was she supposed to look him in the eye—how could she—or was she supposed to close her eyes?

He smiled down at her. "Trust me, Anne."

She nodded and kept her eyes open as he settled between her legs. The warmth of his thighs against hers was far more compelling than the warmth of just his hand. His length bumped her opening. He reached between them and slipped the head of his manhood just inside her folds and she tensed. He lowered his head and brushed his mouth against hers. When he breathed deep, she grasped his arms. Hard muscle flexed beneath her fingers and a thrill shot through her. His hips shifted—then he surged into her. A deep pinch came and went.

Kennedy lifted his mouth from hers and looked down at her. "Are you well?"

Anne nodded, though she wasn't certain. He felt so strange inside her.

He drew back and she gripped his arms tighter in readiness for another pinch when he thrust into her again. None came. He pulled back, then thrust. Kennedy lowered himself onto her and kissed her again, then drove deeper. Pleasure mixed with a smidgen of pain startled her. His tongue slipped inside her mouth. Her head whirled as his thrusts increased speed. Pleasure rippled through her. He drove deeper and the pain increased a little. Still, she was shocked to find she wanted more.

His kiss became insistent. With his next thrust, she lifted her hips. When their bodies collided, he groaned. The sound reverberated through her. Her mother hadn't told her about *any* of this. She also hadn't told her about the pleasure that exploded inside her when her husband drove so deep she thought he'd touched her soul.

～

KENNEDY HAD READ THE PARAGRAPH IN THE REPORT HALF A dozen times and still wasn't certain what it said. His focus kept returning to yesterday afternoon—and last night—with Anne. There was something about her. She excited him. He found he was looking forward to getting to know her in the years that lay ahead. Even with Jacqueline, he'd never considered such a thing. He never thought of being without Jacqueline, but he hadn't thought past what they had, either. With Anne, he found himself looking forward to more afternoons in the conservatory. With Jacqueline, he wanted her, felt he couldn't get enough of her, but he also never felt…satisfied. Anne satisfied him in a way he'd never known possible.

Was this love? He had believed himself to be in love with Jacqueline. The emotions had been intense, but somehow different. He couldn't quite put his finger on it.

A knock came to the door and he started from his thoughts as a footman entered.

"Mr. John Weston to see ye, sir," he said.

John? "Show him in, immediately," Kennedy said, but he didn't have to wait, for John stepped into the room.

Kennedy rose and hurried around his desk toward his friend. John strode toward him and the footman closed the door behind him. They met, clasped hands, and Kennedy said. "What happened? You have learned something."

Surprise shone on John's face.

"What is it?" Kennedy demanded.

"You don't know?"

Kennedy's heart began to pound. "Know what? Tell me, man."

"Your father is in a coma."

The words didn't register. "What? What do you mean?"

"I have a servant in your father's household in my employ," John said. "He just reported that the doctor visited Chesterfield two hours ago because your father wouldn't wake up."

A coma? A dozen thoughts bounced off the inside of his skull, but one word resounded: Rose. What would happen to Rose?

Kennedy looked at his friend. "What if he dies?"

"Sit down, Kennedy."

"What?" Kennedy couldn't focus on his friend's words.

"Sit." John grasped his arm, urged him over to the chair near the window and pushed him onto the seat. John sat on the divan to his right.

"Think, Kennedy. Your sister is safe, at least for now. She has only been away from home for nine days. The situation cannot have degraded in so short a time."

Kennedy nodded. He was right. But how quickly could things degrade now that the earl couldn't send instructions for her safekeeping? He prayed Ranald had luck in finding her in France.

As if reading his mind, John said, "Your father is not a complete fool. He knew you would kill him if anything happened to her. He will have made provisions. She is safe for, at least, some time."

Kennedy nodded. He was right. He had to be right.

"There is more," John said. "I didn't want to say anything until I was certain, but there is no time now to confirm. I suspect that the person your father was using to keep in contact with your sister is a servant within his household."

"What do you mean?"

"As you know, I have had the house watched at all times. Only the usual activity has taken place: food deliveries, supplies, the comings and goings of servants. I doubt any of the deliverymen are anything but what they appear to be. Therefore, it is easy to strike them off the list of potential contacts. That leaves only the servants. I have jested before about how servants know everything, but it is the truth. Someone in your father's household knows something about your sister's whereabouts. My guess is that servant is a man."

Kennedy grunted. "Of that, you can be assured. My father believes women to be weak in all things."

John chuckled. "In that he is very mistaken."

Kennedy nodded. "Have you any idea who the man might be?"

"Your father employs twenty-nine servants. Half of those are women. Half of the men are likely not intelligent enough or reliable enough to be trusted with the passage of information. I have a list of the remaining seven men. I would like you to take a look at the names." He reached inside his pocket and pulled out a folded paper, then handed it to Kennedy.

Kennedy took it and opened it. He scanned the list. "I know three of these men. David Henderson has been my father's stable master for twenty years. He is a possibility. Jason is his valet. He is loyal to my father; however, he would not be my first choice."

"Why?" John asked.

Kennedy shrugged. "My father believes in a strong separation between nobility and servants. To confide in Jason would be to elevate his station as valet."

John nodded. "What about the others?"

"The last name on the list." Kennedy pointed out the name Henry McKinley. "He has worked for my father for two years. In truth, I was surprised my father kept him on. He does not take orders well."

"Interesting," John murmured. "What about the third name on the list, Milton Hayes? He has worked for your father for only two months as a groomsman."

Kennedy shrugged. "I know nothing of him. Are any of these other men new on his staff?"

John nodded. "Aye, the fourth name on the list, Dawson. He has worked as a groomsman for two weeks."

Kennedy leaned back in his chair. "I do not know him. As he is new to my father's staff, perhaps my father hired him specifically to help keep track of Rose." Kennedy looked up at John. "What about his man of affairs, or his solicitor, Mr. Spector?"

"One of them would be an obvious choice," John said. "And your father might fear that you would approach them and try to beat the information out of them."

Kennedy thinned his lips. "He is right."

"However, they could have information without realizing it," John said. "There has to be bills relating to your sister's living expenses."

Kennedy had considered that. "Aye." His heart began to thud. "With my father in a coma, I can demand to see all his financial records."

John nodded. "My thoughts exactly. Ye may also question his servants without fear of repercussions."

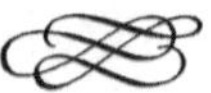

# CHAPTER 9

By that evening, Kennedy had taken possession of all the records he could locate in Mr. Spector's office, as well as the records kept by Mr. Cummins, his father's man of affairs. Mr. Spector had refused to cooperate, but John held a pistol to his head while Kennedy confiscated everything he could find. Mr. Cummins was more cooperative, and handed over two ledgers and a box of receipts.

Kennedy didn't return home, but went to John's office, for he knew that Jacqueline would be waiting for him at home. He was confident that Anne could deal with her. He would make it up to his wife tomorrow. For now, he had to find Rose.

The afternoon turned into evening as he and John poured over files, ledgers and receipts.

"Kennedy."

Kennedy looked up from the ledger he was reading.

"I have never been inside Chesterfield, but it is large," John said.

Kennedy nodded. "Mammoth, in fact."

"Could someone be locked in a room there without the servants knowing?"

Kennedy started. "What are you saying?

John handed him a receipt. Kennedy read the receipt. A lock had been installed on a fourth floor suite in Chesterfield's west wing. Kennedy stared for a long moment before accepting what his eyes told him.

He looked at John. "It's too simple."

"That's the beauty," John said.

"She never left Chesterfield? It can't be."

"Why?"

Kennedy shook his head, unable to focus. "I could find her too easily. The west wing isn't in use. For the most part, it's reserved for guests. My mother spent a year there when she and my father were estranged."

"Then it wouldn't be difficult to lock someone in a room there without the rest of the household knowing," John said.

Kennedy shook his head. "Rose's screams would be heard. My father might trust one or two servants, but, as you said, servants see everything. They would notice."

"Would they notice someone who lived there if that someone didn't mingle with the rest of the household?" John asked.

Kennedy started to answer, then stopped. There were two entrances on that side of the house. Perhaps it could be done if someone were careful. Still... "Once Rose realized she was being held prisoner, she would scream for help," he said.

John's expression softened. "Not if she were incapacitated."

An image flashed of his sweet, dark-haired sister lying in bed, dosed with laudanum. Shock reverberated through him. He'd feared that if he couldn't comply with his father's demands that his father would make good on the threat to marry her to Granbury. He feared the earl would die and Rose would be stranded somewhere in a foreign land with no resources to reach home safely. He had hated not knowing where she was, being uncertain of her future for even a day.

But he had believed that, for the moment, she was safe. Had he been wrong?

"I believed everything he said," Kennedy whispered.

"Why wouldn't you?" John said. "This is more fiendish than sending her away."

Kennedy surged to his feet. "I'm going to Chesterfield."

John stood. "Let's be off."

Kennedy shook his head. "This is not your fight, John."

John clapped him on the back. "I owe you for saving my life in Glasgow." He grinned. "Ye know how much I hate being in debt."

FOR AN HOUR, ANNE SAT ON THE DIVAN IN KENNEDY'S STUDY trying to read before she began to wonder if she was being foolish for waiting. After their encounter in the conservatory yesterday afternoon, he had appeared in her bedchambers later that night and made love to her a second time. But she'd woken to find him gone. After a day shopping with Louisa and her mother, she returned home to find that Kennedy had come and gone. That had been three hours ago. Her mother and Louisa were leaving tomorrow, and Louisa had begged for one last night in town. Mama, had taken her to the opera.

Anne had hoped for time alone with Kennedy, again. Her cheeks warmed at the thought. Would he think her loose now? Was a wife supposed to enjoy her husband so much? He certainly seemed to enjoy his time with her. Was this what she had to look forward to for the rest of her life? "

What had his father said? *"It hadn't occurred to me you might be beautiful, but the fact that you are will hold Kennedy's interest for a while."* If his father spoke the truth, how long before Kennedy tired of her? What would she do when he took other lovers? I thought struck. Did he have a mistress? Her heart sank. Of course, he did. A man like him always had a mistress.

She was a fool. He bore no particular affection for her. He only married because his father commanded that he sire an heir as quickly as possible. Perhaps he was enjoying himself in the process. Perhaps once their son was born, he would lose interest in her altogether.

He wasn't home because he had no interest in seeing her, and here she was waiting for him in his study. Thank God, he hadn't come home and found her waiting. Not only would she feel like a fool, she would look like a fool. She closed her book and rose. A knock sounded on the door, then the door opened and the butler entered.

"Forgive me, my lady, but there is a boy here who insists upon seeing his lordship."

"Kennedy isn't here," she said.

"I am aware he is no' at home," Mr. Bingham said. "But the boy insists that he will not leave until he has seen Lord Buchanan."

"What does he want with the viscount?" she asked.

Mr. Bingham shook his head. "He refuses to say. "

"Perhaps he will tell me. Show him in, please."

He bowed and left. Anne sat back down on the divan and, a moment later, Mr. Bingham returned with a tall lad of about fourteen years of age, dressed in britches and a rough woolen coat. He reminded her of a stable hand.

Anne remain seated as the boy approached. "I am Lady Anne," she said. "What is this message you have for my husband?"

The boy stopped near the table in front of the divan. "It's from his sister," he said.

"His sister?" Anne snapped her gaze onto the butler, who was closing the door. "Mr. Bingham, wait, please."

He paused. "Yes, ma'am?"

"Does his lordship have a sister?"

"Aye, my lady. Lady Rose. She lives with the earl."

Why hadn't Kennedy mentioned her? Why hadn't she attended their wedding? Why hadn't they met her at the ball? She hesitated. She needed to hear what the boy had to say, but she felt completely lost.

"Mr. Bingham, will you wait outside the door, please?"

"Of course, my lady." He stepped into the hallway, pulling the door closed behind him.

Anne returned her attention to the boy. "What is your name?"

"Matthew, my lady."

She smiled. "Matthew, what is the message?"

The boy stubbornly shook his head. "Lady Rose specifically instructed me to tell no one but her brother."

Anne pinned him with a hard stare. "I assume the message is important or you wouldn't be here refusing to leave."

"Aye, ma'am, very important.

"Too important to delay in delivering?" she pressed.

His brows knit in uncertainty. "It's devilish important—begging your pardon, my lady."

"Never mind that," she said. "I'm sure Lady Rose thought his lordship would be home. But he isn't, and we can't say when he will return. If it's important, perhaps ye had better tell me. I am his wife, so there is little difference between telling him and telling me." Normally, she wasn't nosy, but intense curiosity—and more than a little frustration—made her want to hear the message.

The young man considered. "I suppose ye might be right. Lady Rose sounded very desperate." His expression grew serious. "But if I tell you, I must still tell his lordship." He stood straighter. "I promised, and a gentleman never breaks his word to a lady."

Anne smiled. "Of course, you are absolutely correct. Please

tell me the message, then I will have Mr. Bingham take you to the kitchen where Mrs. Hampshire will fix you tea and something to eat. You may wait until his lordship arrives, then repeat to him the message, as well."

His eyes brightened. "I am hungry, ma'am."

"Then you shall have a fine dinner. Will that do?"

He gave a concise nod. "Yes, ma'am. The young lady asked me to tell his lordship that she is being held prisoner in Chesterfield Hall."

Anne blinked. "Being held prisoner? Surely, there must be some mistake?"

He shook his head. "I said the same thing. How can anyone be a prisoner in their own home? I didn't want to call a lady a liar, but I did accuse her of making fun of me. Then she showed me bruises on her cheek and arm. She is telling the truth. I'm sure if it."

"She is being beat?" Anne asked. It was simply too fantastical.

"Aye, so you can see how I would have to believe her."

Anne nodded. "That is serious proof." But could she believe him?

"Lady Rose was very specific," he went on. "She said his lordship was to come to her by way of the west entrance, and she begged him to hurry."

"If she's being held captive, how is it you came to speak with her?"

"My father has the best milk and butter in all of Edinburgh. The earl buys our butter and milk. I was making the delivery when I passed by the window and she called to me. I must tell you the truth, though. Lady Rose told me that I must be honest. She promised that I would not get into trouble."

"If Lady Rose promised you would not get into trouble, then you shall not get into trouble." Anne studied him. "Did she promise you money for delivering the message?"

His chin lifted. "She did, but a gentleman never takes money for helping a lady in distress."

"You are right again," Anne murmured. "What is this truth you must tell me?"

"Normally, I go around the side to the servants' entrances on the east. But that's a longer walk, and I was in a hurry. So I climbed the wall and cut through on that side of the estate."

"I have seen that wall," Anne said. "It's very high."

He gave her a disparaging look. "I can easily climb it. It would be difficult if I was delivering milk because milk spills. But this time I was only delivering butter, and butter doesn't spill. It was very fortunate I took that route, according to Lady Rose, for she said no one ever came across the estate on that side."

"Did Lady Rose say why she was being held captive?"

He shook his head. "Eight days maybe. She wasn't certain."

Since last Saturday or Sunday, Anne thought. One or two days before she received the summons from the earl. That was odd.

"She said the lady who watches her is evil," Matthew said.

"Evil?" Anne repeated. "Is it she who beats Lady Rose?"

"I don't know. She did say the woman gave her laudanum to keep her quiet, but Lady Rose promised not to scream, so she didn't give her as much."

The story was too preposterous. Oh, how she wished Kennedy were here, or even her mother. "When his lordship returns home, you can repeat the story for him," Anne said.

Matthew nodded. "I hope he returns soon. Lady Rose over-heard the evil woman speaking with the man who brings them their food. He said that the earl was very ill and they thought he might die soon."

That Anne knew to be true. The earl didn't look at all well.

"He has fallen into a coma," the boy said.

"A coma?" she blurted. She had heard no such thing. Surely,

Kennedy would tell her if that were true. Might that be why he'd been gone all afternoon?

"I did not know anything else," he said. "Except Lady Rose is very afraid they will send her away now that the earl is dying."

"Send her away where?"

"She didn't say, she only said that she must be away for nine months or more. They said something about his lordship having a child."

Anne stared. The boy would have absolutely no reason to make up something like that.

# CHAPTER 10

ANNE HAD MR. BINGHAM TAKE MATTHEW TO THE KITCHEN FOR a good dinner, where he would wait until Kennedy returned home. A messenger was sent to the boy's home that explained where he was—Anne swore Matthew to secrecy in regards to 'the lady's message' as he now referred to his mission. Then she asked Mr. Bingham about Lady Rose and learned that Kennedy's sister was fifteen years old, and she and Kennedy were very close. Though Mr. Bingham stated that it wasn't his place to comment, he did admit that he was surprised that Lady Rose hadn't joined them for the wedding and the bridal feast that followed, or that she hadn't been to visit in over a week. He didn't know where Kennedy had gone, and Kennedy hadn't left word when he might return. It was eight twenty, and her mother would not return for another two hours, at least.

She waited another hour, but when Kennedy didn't arrive home, she spoke once again with Matthew and learned which window he had seen Lady Rose in. Then she ordered the carriage brought around, and changed into a plain dress and cloak. As she clasped the footman's hand in preparation to enter the carriage, someone called her name. She paused and looked back to find Matthew bounding down the stairs toward her.

He reached the carriage and said between breaths, "You are going to rescue her, aren't ye, my lady?"

"I am going to see what I can learn about the situation," she said in a quiet voice.

The boy cast the footman a glance, then said, "I will come with you."

"Nae," she said. "Someone must wait here to speak with my husband when he returns. That is your job, Matthew."

He shook his head stubbornly. "That is a baby's job. I am a man. Ye can leave word with Mr. Bingham. But I am going with you, my lady. It is not right that you should go without a man to protect you."

Heaven save her from the men who wanted to protect her. "You will stay here, Matthew."

But before she could say more, he shrugged. "I can get there on my own, just as I came here."

"How did you come here?" she asked.

"I have a horse. I took her to your stables. But I can have her saddled in two minutes. A horse is much faster than a carriage, and I know a shortcut."

Anne sighed. "Then I suppose you will come with me. However, you will do exactly as I say."

He shrugged. The footman helped her into the carriage, then Matthew leapt inside and settled on the seat opposite her.

When the carriage was two blocks from the earl's estate, she had the driver stop. Of course, despite her commands, Matthew insisted on coming. James, also, refused to allow her to walk alone in the dark, and they left the footman with the carriage while they set out.

They reached the east wall that Matthew had climbed over to cut across Chesterfield's lawn. When they turned the street corner, Anne said, "James, I know this is an odd request, but

I'm asking that you wait outside the gate while I continue on. I'll be safe enough once we're on the earl's estate."

He nodded, but she knew he wondered what she was up to. At least, with Matthew present, James wouldn't think she was meeting another gentleman.

They reached the wrought iron gate, which stood open. James remained at the entrance. Anne pulled her cloak tighter about her as she and Matthew kept walking. A dim light shown in a ground floor window at the front of the house, which Anne guessed to be a parlor. Another light flickered in a third-floor window. That, she estimated to be the earl's bed chambers. Thankfully, the curtains were drawn. More soft line shone in two windows on the top floor where the servants would be.

They hurried around the drive on the right side of the house, then slowed. This side of the house was completely dark, except for a meager light that flickered against closed drapes in a fourth story window.

"That's the window," James whispered.

Anne's heart began to pound. Was his story really true? On the carriage ride, she'd considered half a dozen explanations for his story, not the least of which, that he knew just enough of current events to have fabricated the tale. She had to admit, his story contained some strange coincidences. Rose claimed to have been kidnapped just about the time she met Kennedy. But what could her meeting and marriage to Kennedy have to do with his sister? And how could someone claim to be kidnapped while still living in their home? It wouldn't really be called kidnapping. But a woman could be held prisoner in her own home.

Now that they were here, she had no idea how she would go about proving the truth, one way or the other. She scanned the wall for a door. There would be some sort of entrance on the side of the house. Of course, that door would be locked. She spotted a door farther down the side of the building, and hurried forward. As expected, it was locked.

It was only ten-thirty. Despite the light in the earl's room, he would likely be asleep. Jacqueline, too, was probably abed. Most of the servants would take advantage of the quiet and would retire to their rooms or go to bed, for they would have to rise early to complete their morning duties. Still, a few servants might be in the kitchen working or socializing.

When they turned the corner of the building she saw another door, this one smaller than the last. The other door they'd seen, while a side entrance, was clearly for visitors. This door, however, was a rear servants' entrance. She tried the knob and was surprised when it turned. Slowly, she inched the door open. Enough moonlight illuminated the room for her to recognize some sort of pantry. On a shelf to the left, sat several tapers and a tinder box. This entrance was in use.

Anne entered and lit a candle, then faced Matthew and whispered, "Remain here."

"I cannae let you go alone, my lady. I am responsible for you."

"Do you disobey your mother like this?" she asked in frustration.

"I never knew my mother," he said. "She died when I was little. It's just me and my father."

That explained much. She should have had the footman carry Matthew back to the house and tie him to a chair, but she hadn't thought of it. Anne turned and he followed as she crept forward and entered a modest kitchen. This section of the mansion clearly was intended for someone who might want to live away from the main part of the house. She located service stairs immediately to the right and they climbed to the fourth floor. Anne halted at sight of the tiny sliver of light shining into the pitch black hallway from beneath a door up ahead.

Her heart began to pound. What should she do? If Lady

Rose was in the room—and if her warden was with her—how would she help the girl? Should she return home and wait for Kennedy? Should she rouse someone in the house, the earl or his wife?

She looked at Matthew, who nodded toward the light. Anne nodded acknowledgement and they crept to the door. She knocked lightly. Silence followed. With a deep breath, she grasped the knob and slowly twisted it. To her surprise, the knob turned. Why would they leave the door unlocked if they were keeping the girl prisoner? If Rose had lied—or if Matthew had lied—then she was making a huge mistake by being here.

Her hand shook, but she forced calm and eased the door open. First, she caught sight of a table and two chairs that sat before a hearth wherein a low fire burned. A tea pot and two cups sat on the table, along with a sugar bowl and cream. No one cried out, and Anne stepped into the room. To the left, sat a fourposter bed. A young woman lay in the bed, the blankets pulled up beneath her arms.

"Excuse me," Anne called, but the girl didn't reply.

Anne whispered to Matthew, "This is a lady's room. You remain here while I wake her."

Thankfully, he nodded agreement this time. She crossed to the bed and drew a sharp breath at sight of the bruise on the girl's cheek. Matthew hadn't lied. Anne set her taper on the nightstand, then grasped the girl's shoulder and gently shook her.

The girl's eyes fluttered open and her brow knit. "Rebecca?" The word was slurred, as if she had ingested laudanum.

Anger shot through Anne. Here was the reason they hadn't locked the door. The girl couldn't stand, much less escape.

"I am Kennedy's wife," Anne said.

Her frown deepened. "Kennedy? Is he here?" A tear slid down the side of her face.

Anne's heart constricted. "Can you tell me what has happened?"

Rose squeezed her eyes closed and more tears fell.

"Are you being held against your will?"

Her eyes shot open. "Rebecca will return and she will be angry."

"Shh, I am here," Anne soothed. "You have nothing to fear." Anne wasn't at all certain that was true.

Rose began to whimper.

"Matthew," Anne called, "bring me a cup of that tea on the table."

While he did as she ordered, Anne pulled the covers back, swung Rose's legs off the side of the bed and pulled her into a sitting position. Matthew appeared with the tea.

"I'll hold her upright while you get her to drink the tea," Anne said.

He complied, and they forced half the tea down her throat before Rose twisted her head aside.

"Come on, love," Anne coaxed, "drink more."

They got another couple of good swallows into her with the rest dribbling down her chin. Anne had no idea how much laudanum this Rebecca had given her, but she gave thanks that wasn't enough for the girl to be unconscious. She had seen people given enough laudanum that they didn't wake for twelve hours.

Anne grasped Rose's chin, forcing the girl to look at her. "Can you walk?"

Her brow knit as if she were trying to understand Anne's words.

"Do you want to leave this place?" Anne asked.

Understanding lit her clouded eyes and she nodded.

"Good." Anne whipped off her cloak and swung it around Rose's shoulders, then fastened the clasp. "Come on, let's see if you can stand."

Anne pulled her to her feet. Rose swayed. Anne feared she would topple back onto the bed. Matthew grasped her arm and steadied her. The lad had been more right than Anne realized. She needed his help—Rose needed him. She was thankful when he slipped an arm around Rose's waist and took most of her weight. Anne picked up the taper and they walked with her across the room and out into the hall. How would they get her down the stairs without all of them falling and breaking their necks?

Anne came to an abrupt halt at the sound of approaching footfalls behind them. She twisted and looked over her shoulder. Light flickered around the bend up ahead and a woman rounded the corner in the next instant. She took three steps before seeing them, then shrieked and tossed her candle aside as she raced toward them.

Anne faced forward. They were too far from the stairs to have any chance of outrunning her. "Matthew, can you get Rose safely down the stairs?"

"Aye, my lady. I am very strong."

Anne prayed he was. "Get her down the stairs and out to James—quick.

"I cannot leave you, my lady," he said.

Anne released Rose and Matthew hugged her closer. "You must save the lady," she hissed. "I can take care of myself. She is just a woman." Anne whirled.

Their attacker might be just a woman, but she was a woman racing toward them as if the devil nipped at her heels—a women who stood a head taller than her.

Candle in hand, Anne walked quickly toward her. An instant later, she was within ten feet of the woman and stopped in the middle of the hallway. "Halt, madam. I am Viscountess Buchanan, the Earl of Buchanan's daughter-in-law."

The woman stopped so quickly she stumbled forward two paces before catching herself.

"What are you doing with my husband's sister?" Anne demanded.

The woman's eyes flicked past her and came back her face. "You are not supposed to be here." She started forward as if to hurry past Anne's left side, but Anne slid into her path.

The woman halted. "Out of my way," she growled.

"My husband will not be pleased that you mistreated his sister, Rebecca," Anne said.

Fear flickered in her eyes, then was followed by fury. Anne noted the subtle change in her stance and realized the woman was about to charge. Rebecca lunged. Anne whipped aside and stuck out her foot as she hurtled past. Rebecca stumbled, hands out, and crashed into the wall. She dropped to the carpet and lay motionless.

Anne retreated two paces, heart pounding, knees so weak she feared they would give out. Bootfalls echoed from the direction Rebecca had come. Anne whirled and raced down the hallway in the opposite direction. She reached the stairs and was forced to slow in the pitch darkness. A hand on each wall of the narrow staircase, she forced herself to slow, and prayed her legs wouldn't give out.

At the bottom, she gave thanks that Matthew and Rose were nowhere to be seen, then hurried through the kitchen pantry and out into the cool night. She pumped her legs faster and reached the front of the house in seconds. She nearly cried, at sight of Matthew and Rose passing through the wrought-iron gate where James stood.

A moment later, Anne reached the wrought-iron gate then turned and nearly collided with Matthew. "Dear Lord," she burst out. "What are you doing here?"

"James is assisting Lady Rose," Matthew said. "I couldnae leave you there alone."

She grabbed his arm and pulled him into a run.

A shout went up somewhere near the house. They sprinted

around the corner. Anne thought her lungs would burst, but she kept going. They reached the carriage. She didn't wait for help, but grasped the door and jumped inside and onto the seat beside Rose.

"Hurry, James, we must go *now.*"

Matthew leapt inside, pulling the door closed behind him.

Anne pulled Rose close as the carriage tilted left, then jolted into motion hard enough for to have to grab onto the handle. Rose cried into Anne's bodice and Anne willed herself not to burst into tears herself.

# CHAPTER 11

KENNEDY GUIDED HIS HORSE UP THE DRIVE TO CHESTERFIELD, with John riding alongside. They continued around the east side of the house to the rear, and Kennedy brought the animal to a halt at sight of the open servants' entrance. He leapt from the saddle and raced inside. He knew this part of the house like the back of his hand. When his mother had been alive, they often entertained guests here. After her death, Kennedy spent many a day in the deserted rooms.

Kennedy spotted the tapers and tinderbox on the pantry shelf, and cursed.

A shadow filled the doorway. "Someone is using this entrance," John said.

Kennedy's gut clenched. *Rose is here.*

He forced back the compulsion to race up the darkened stairs. He was no longer fifteen. The narrow staircase was pitch black at night and he was sure to break his fool neck.

He lit a candle, and said to John, "Come on," then hurried from the pantry into the kitchen and took the stairs to the right.

They reached the fourth floor. Light spilled from an open

door halfway down the hallway. He blew out the candle, tossed it aside, and raced toward the open door. He and John burst inside the room to find a man sitting on the mattress beside a woman.

"*Rose*," Kennedy growled, and took two steps toward the man before strong fingers seized his arm and yanked him back.

"That is not Rose," John said.

For an instant, Kennedy didn't understand, then he whipped his head around and looked at the couple. The man stood, staring at them. The woman was not Rose.

Not Rose. Where was his sister?

Kennedy yanked free of John and said to the man, "Where is my sister?"

He shook his head. "I dinnae know. I returned to find Rebecca unconscious in the hallway."

Kennedy rounded the bed, then took the woman by the shoulders. Her head lolled to the side. He shook her.

"Leave her be!" the man shouted.

Kennedy yanked his gaze onto the man and he backed up two steps. Kennedy looked back at the woman and she shook her again.

John appeared at his side. "Here, maybe this will help." He tossed water from a pitcher onto the woman's face.

She sputtered and shook her head. Her eyes snapped open. Her gaze met Kennedy's and her eyes widened.

"Where is my sister?" he demanded.

She looked at the man.

Kennedy gave her a hard shake. "Where is Lady Rose?"

"A woman took her."

Panic muddled his thoughts. "A woman? What woman? Where did she take her?"

"She-she said she was Lady Buchanan."

"Lady Buchanan?" he repeated. "Jacqueline?"

"N-nae," the woman stuttered. "Viscountess Buchanan, Lady Rose's sister-in-law."

"Anne?" Had he heard correctly? "My wife was here?"

The woman's eyes widened. "You are Viscount Buchanan?" She shrank away from him.

He released her and straightened. "You are certain it was Viscountess Buchanan who was here?"

She nodded vigorously. "She had a lad with her. She tripped me and I hit the wall." The woman turned her head to the side and showed him the bruise forming on her forehead.

Kennedy could hardly credit it. He looked at John. "What the bloody hell was my wife doing here?"

John shook his head. "I can't imagine."

Kennedy looked at the man. "Who are you?"

"Angus Dunning. I bring food to Rebecca while she is tending to the young lady."

"What you mean 'tending to the young lady'?"

"Her father didn't want to put her into an insane asylum," Rebecca said. "So, he paid me to care for her here. He said it was better than the insane asylum," she quickly added. "He is very kind."

"Kind?" Kennedy snarled. "We shall see if that defense holds up in court." He looked at John. "I must return home. Will you keep them here until I return?"

"Here, now," Angus said. "There's no call to treat us like criminals. We were paid to take care of the young lady for her father. Rebecca and I can leave anytime we like."

John flashed white teeth. "You are free to try, lad."

Kennedy glimpsed the man's wide eyes an instant before he whirled and strode from the room.

· · ·

Kennedy reached home half an hour later and leapt off his horse almost before the beast stopped. He bounded up the steps and banged the knocker until the door was yanked open.

"Whoever you are—" Bingham broke off. "I beg your pardon, my lord. I didn't realize—"

Kennedy pushed past him. "Where is my wife?"

"In the Burgundy guest chamber, sir, with Lady Rose."

"My sister is here?" he said in a harsh whisper.

Bingham nodded. "Aye," he replied, but Kennedy was already racing up the stairs.

He burst into the Burgundy guest chambers to find Anne standing with her mother and sister while the doctor sat on the bed, blocking view of his patient.

Kennedy took a step forward. "Rose?"

The doctor stood, and Rose cried, "Kennedy!"

Kennedy drew a sharp breath. His sister sat propped up in bed, her left cheek, yellowed with a bruise. He strode across the room to the bed, fell to his knees and pulled her to him. She threw her arms around his neck and he buried his face in her neck and wept.

Anne felt Kennedy's eyes on her for the dozenth time as she and Matthew related their tale, but she kept her gaze on her hands clasped in her lap. Louisa sat between her and her mother on the divan in the drawing room, for Louisa refused to be sent to bed. Kennedy sat in the chair to the left, as Matthew continued his story.

"Her ladyship refused to leave with Lady Rose and I," Matthew said, and Anne winced.

"What did she do?" her husband asked.

"She stayed to fight the evil woman while Lady Rose and I escaped."

From the corner of her eye, she saw Kennedy stare at her again.

"Was that when you tripped her?" Kennedy asked.

Anne looked sharply at him. "How do you know that?"

"I had a talk with Rebecca."

"Oh," she said, and fell silent again.

"I got Lady Rose outside to James," Matthew went on. "Then her ladyship came, and we were able to escape." Matthew stood straighter, as if waiting for further instructions.

Kennedy rose and extended his hand to the lad. "I owe you more than I can ever repay."

The boy looked up at him in surprise then clasped Kennedy's hand and they shook.

"Name any price," Kennedy said, "and it is yours."

Anne hid a smile when Matthew said, "A gentleman never takes money for rescuing a lady."

Kennedy stared, as if uncertain what to say, then nodded. "When Rose is better, we would consider it an honor if you would join us for dinner. She will want to thank you personally."

Startlement flashed across the boy's face, then he said in a solemn voice, "It would be my honor."

A knock came to the door and Mr. Bingham entered." A message has arrived for you, my lord." He crossed to Kennedy and handed him a note, then waited.

Kennedy scanned the note, which was from John, stating that the constable Kennedy had sent for had arrived at Chesterfield. He had Rebecca and Angus in custody, and Kennedy was to appear in the morning to make formal charges.

Kennedy looked at Bingham. "Bingham, please send a note to John with my thanks, and tell him I will visit him tomorrow."

Bingham bowed, then left.

"Matthew," Kennedy said, "my carriage will take you home."

"There is no need for that. I have a horse."

Kennedy shook his head. "Indulge me in this, lad. I would rest easier if my coach takes you. I will direct the driver to pick you up tomorrow so that you may retrieve your horse in daylight hours."

"If that is what you wish, my lord."

"You didn't obey me so easily," Anne said under her breath.

The boy looked at her in surprise. "Of course not, my lady. What you asked me to do was impossible."

"Ahh," she intoned. "I forget myself. You were supposed to protect me…and Lady Rose." She smiled. "I don't know what I would've done without you." It wasn't a lie. "Thank you."

He bowed, and Kennedy directed him to tell Mr. Bingham to have a carriage brought around. Matthew left, then her mother stood and said, "Come along, Louisa. It's late."

"But, Mama."

"No arguments," their mother cut in. "Come along." She looked at Kennedy. "We are very happy your sister is home, Kennedy."

He nodded, and said in a hoarse voice, "Thank you, my lady."

She smiled gently and said, "Perhaps you should call me, Christina." Then she and Louisa left Anne alone with her husband.

Anne didn't know why, but she was suddenly terrified.

Kennedy stared at her. "What sort of woman are you?"

She looked at him. "I don't understand."

"You hardly know me. You don't know Rose, at all. Yet you put yourself in jeopardy to save her."

Anne shrugged. "When I saw her, the situation she was in, it was clear she was being held against her will. I couldn't leave her there."

"You could've come to me. You could have not gone at all and let Matthew tell me his story when I returned home."

"Matthew said Lady Rose feared that they were going to take her away. In truth, my lord, I couldn't credit that the story was true. But there were enough truths that I couldn't ignore the possibility that the tale might be true." She hesitated, and said, "Why did your father have her locked up?"

His mouth thinned. "Are you sure you want to know the answer? You won't like it."

"Of course, I won't like it. There is nothing that justifies locking someone up, much less one's own child." Her blood boiled at the memory of finding the girl half out of her mind with the laudanum, and clearly physically abused.

"That isn't what I mean," Kennedy said. "The reason concerns you—our marriage."

She frowned, then comprehension dawned. "You mean your father used her to force you to marry me? How— I-I don't understand."

"My father told me that he had Rose taken away. I believed he had taken her from Scotland. Sent her to France, perhaps. Had I the slightest idea she was still in Edinburgh, in her own home—" His hands worked into fists at his sides.

Anne could well understand his anger and panic. She couldn't imagine anything happening to Louisa.

"He demanded I marry immediately and produce an heir," Kennedy said.

Anne nodded. He'd been right. She didn't want to know. She'd known the earl had instigated the marriage. Yet, somehow, this knowledge tainted their union in a way she couldn't describe.

She looked at her hands, still clasped in her lap. "I am so sorry." Tears pressed at the backs of her eyes. "Of course, we cannot remain married."

"What?" he said sharply.

She snapped her head up.

He crossed to her and stopped beside the divan. "We've been married three days. I need time to learn how to be a husband. Surely, you will give me more time."

She looked at him in confusion. "We married because your father held your sister captive. I-I cannot imagine how you can even stand to look at me."

"Quite the contrary. I cannot bear the thought of not seeing your face every day for the rest of my life."

She blinked. "What? I don't understand. Our marriage—"

He grasped her arm and pulled her to her feet. "Is the best thing that ever happened to me. I am sorry, my dear, but I have no intention of letting you go."

Before she could reply, he kissed her until she couldn't think straight.

# EPILOGUE

KENNEDY'S FATHER DIED THE FOLLOWING EVENING. THREE DAYS
later, Kennedy gave Jacqueline his townhouse and moved his
new family into Chesterfield Hall. It would take a month for all
their belongings to be brought over. But he cared not. He had
grown up in this house. His mother had died in this house. His
sister had been imprisoned and then rescued in this house.
Lastly, he would never forget that even his father had died in
this house. This was where they belonged.

The dowager viscountess returned to Dover Hall, and left
Louisa with them. Two months had passed. In another week,
they would go to Dover Hall for the summer. By the time they
returned home, Anne would be entering her sixth month of
pregnancy and they would settle in until the birth of their
child.

Light footfalls sounded outside his study, then the door
burst open and Louisa and Rose rushed in.

Rose waved a note card. "We have been invited to a lawn
party this afternoon. Please say we may go."

"It's up to Anne," he said.

"Where is she?" Louisa asked.

Kennedy stood. He would guess, in the conservatory. "I will find her."

He left the girls and went to the conservatory. This conservatory was twice the size of the one in his townhouse. He entered and ambled to the rear of the room where, as expected, he found his wife lying on the chaise that he had put there in front of the hearth, where only embers burned. A book lay open across her stomach, which had yet to show signs of the life growing inside of her. But she was napping. Something she did a little more often now than she used to—at least, according to her.

He put another log on the fire, then stood and turned to find her staring at him.

"This is my favorite room in the house," she said.

He lifted a brow. "Your favorite room?"

She shrugged. "Perhaps my second favorite."

He went to the chaise and sat beside her. "Perhaps you would like to spend a little time in your favorite room with me."

She released a contented sigh. "Why move when this is such a comfortable chaise?"

He smoothed back a lock that had escaped her chignon. "Our sisters want to attend a lawn party this afternoon."

She scooted over and patted the empty place beside her. He stretched out and pulled her against his chest.

She snuggled close and his heart constricted. "How is it I came to be so fortunate as to find you?" he asked.

"You're a very lucky person, I suppose," she murmured."

He supposed that was true. He closed his eyes and drew in a deep breath. "I imagine we should let the girls go to the party."

She nodded against his chest. "We shall never hear the end of it if we don't."

"Do we have to tell them now?"

Anne shifted and pulled his mouth down to hers. "Only if you really want to," she said against his lips.

The only thing he wanted to do was make love to his wife. "Have I told you that I love you?" he said.

She nibbled on his bottom lip. "Only three other times today."

He tightened his arms around her. "I am falling behind. I love you."

She bit a little harder and he suddenly wanted her badly.

"Good," she said. "Because I love you, too."

# SNEAK PEEK AT A
# SCOUNDREL IN THE MAKING

# A Scoundrel in the Making

The Marriage Maker
Book Nine
The Marriage Maker Goes Undercover

Tarah Scott

*Wanted: Gentleman turned rogue...*

Retired spy Abigail Matheson has inherited the title of Marchioness of Buchman upon the death of her cousin. The title, which he'd inherited from her father, should never have been hers. But that annoyance is forgotten when The Raven, Abigail's superior, introduces her to Sir Stirling James. They request her assistance on one final mission: find the stolen crown jewels of Scotland.

Abigail accepts this unexpected opportunity in hopes of forgetting the young French spy she killed on her last assignment. When The Raven and Sir Stirling inform her that she will be working with Lord Reade, a rake of the first order, Abigail, who's always worked alone, plans to ignore the partnership and complete this mission alone.

Lord Reade, brother to Robert Murdock, the Earl of Kinwall, has been given the opportunity to gamble with men who can afford to lose a lot of money. And a lot of money is exactly what Reade needs if he is to save his family's ancestral home from creditors and prevent his brother's family from being forced onto the streets. The catch: he must work with a beautiful spy to find the thief who stole the Honors of Scotland. Surely, he can ignore her long enough to salvage his family's fortune. The string of suitors determined to be the next Marquess of Buchman prove too much a distraction, however, and Reade is forced to take matters into his own hands.

# CHAPTER 1

ABIGAIL SIPPED HER THIRD GLASS OF CHAMPAGNE AND CASUALLY
scanned Lady Bingley's crowded ballroom. Extravagant balls
such as this were as natural to her as breathing—if she were
attending as Lady Abigail, wayward daughter of the Marquess
of Buchman, or even as Carlotta Durand, daughter of Richard
Durand, wealthy French merchant. Attending a ball as Lady
Abigail, *dutiful* daughter of John Matheson, the Marquess of
Buchman, was another matter.

Here in Inverness, she was just a marquess's daughter—
well, more than that now. Six weeks ago, her cousin, the most
recent Marquess of Buchman, went and died of a fever. As a
result, Abigail had become the Marchioness of Buchman, heir
to her father's title, lands and money—and all the headaches
that position entailed. The transition from spy to marchioness
had come as a shock.

Melancholia chilled her heart. Even after five years, she
missed her father so badly her heart ached. When her cousin
Daniel had inherited the title, she'd married Iain Young, intent
on never returning to the memories of Lochland Manor. A
year after their marriage, her husband got himself shot

gambling in a hell, and then six weeks past, Daniel died. His Majesty *might* not insist she marry, but he wasn't keen on the new Marchioness of Buchman risking her life as a spy. Returning home without her father present had been like plunging a knife through her heart.

Abigail finished her champagne and searched for a waiter. At half past twelve, the night was young. The ball would continue at least till two, perhaps even three a.m. By the time she left, she very well might be drunk.

Her gaze snagged on the lead violinist of the orchestra, a strikingly handsome man. How long since she'd indulged in anything tall, dark and handsome?

"That is your third glass of champagne," her friend Fanny said.

At last, a waiter appeared. Abigail stopped him, set her empty glass on the tray, took a full glass, then waved him on.

She faced Fanny. "Who's counting?"

"Clearly, not you."

Abigail sipped the champagne. "And I shan't begin now."

"You're worried that when you marry, your husband will put a stop to your wild ways."

Abigail laughed. "I have only just returned to Scotland. The last thing on my mind is marriage. Besides, my first marriage was quite enough."

Fanny sipped her champagne—as every lady should—and peered at Abigail over the rim of her glass. "The widow of Mr. Young may choose not to remarry, but His Majesty will have something to say about the Marchioness of Buchman not marrying."

Abigail shrugged. Her particular relationship with His Majesty would save her from the marriage mart.

Fanny leaned close and whispered, "Don't look now, but I believe the owner of your next dance is on the way to claim his set."

Abigail frowned. Which dance was this? The fourth. Good God, Viscount Havisham had signed her dance card for the fourth dance. Fanny nodded ever so slightly at something behind Abigail. She turned casually and caught sight of the viscount plowing his way through the crowd. God help her. Abigail faced Fanny.

Fanny's eyes twinkled. "I have heard that a lady who dances with Lord Havisham…well, her toes are never quite the same afterwards."

Abigail narrowed her eyes. "You have a perverse streak, Fanny."

She nodded, her expression neutral, but her eyes flashed with devilish delight. "One would think the reason was because my parents didn't love me. But in fact, they loved me very much."

Abigail bit back a laugh—and a retort—for the gentleman in question had reached hearing distance. At first opportunity, she would speak with Lady Bingley. Abigail had arrived at the ball to find her hostess had filled her dance card. Clearly, Lady Bingley had taken it upon herself to find Abigail a suitable husband.

Lord Havisham reached them, out of breath after his charge across the room. "My lady, I believe the next set is mine."

Abigail glimpsed laughter in Fanny's eyes an instant before her friend dropped her gaze. Abigail suddenly had the suspicion that it wasn't only Lady Bingley playing matchmaker. Fanny's delight was more than mere amusement at Abigail's expense. One would think that Fanny had better taste than to pair Abigail with a portly viscount who probably had never walked farther than the distance between his carriage and his club. Lady Bingley wasn't the only person Abigail needed to set straight. Longing rose for ballrooms where men sought to charm their way into a woman's bed, not drag her down the aisle.

Abigail assumed a wilted expression and fanned her face with her hand. "Sir, it is intolerably hot in here." As expected, his eyes brightened. He believed she intended to ask him to escort her to the balcony. The poor fool. She lowered her voice, "Would you mind very much if I asked a favor?"

"Of course not, my dear." He started to angle his arm toward her.

"Would you fetch me some champagne?"

He blinked. "I beg pardon? Champagne?" He glanced at the glass in her hand.

She smiled. "This champagne is warm. Cool champagne does wonders for a body, do you not agree?" She leaned toward him an inch and added in a sultry voice that had yet to fail her, "It always puts me in the best of moods."

He straightened as if he were a puppet and the puppeteer had yanked his strings. "Indeed, my lady, it would be my pleasure." He looked around the room for a passing waiter. As Abigail knew was the case, no waiter was visible. Indecision creased his brow.

"The champagne in the refreshments room is always the coolest." Abigail looked up at him with adoring eyes. "The party is a crush. Can you reach the refreshments room and return unscathed?"

His indecision lingered for another instant, then manly pride surfaced. "Of course. For you, it is no trouble."

She sighed in genuine relief. "You are too kind."

He bowed, then turned and began to plow his way toward the refreshments room, located on the other side of the large ballroom.

"By the time he returns, the set will be over," Fanny said.

*And I will be gone,* Abigail thought. There were two more parties she could attend tonight. She needn't return home before two, if she chose. She cast a glance at the violinist. Even those broad shoulders weren't worth Havisham's company for the night.

"Wherever did you learn to make such awful moon eyes?" Fanny asked. "I expected him to drop to one knee and profess undying love, then offer to slay any dragon you named."

Abigail finished her champagne. Glass number four. "You are one to talk. I seem to remember you insisting that Charles bring you cakes from downtown Inverness during the heat of an August day."

Fanny shrugged. "That was different. I was in love with Charles."

Abigail grimaced. "Lucky Charles."

Fanny narrowed her eyes. "You know what I mean."

"Indeed, I do. You wanted to see how long the poor fellow would let you torture him before he cried foul."

Fanny gave small shrug. "Something like that."

Abigail lifted a brow. "How long did it take?"

A mischievous grin tugged the corners of Fanny's mouth. "I'll let you know when he does so."

Abigail's gaze snagged on a woman who paused near the hallway to the refreshments room. What was Lady Elana Galloway doing in Inverness—at this party? They'd last parted in Paris. Something was wrong. Abigail hadn't expected to ever again see the spymaster known as The Raven.

Lady Elana turned, started down the hallway, and disappeared from view. Abigail returned her attention to Fanny. Her plans had changed. No more champagne. She would need her wits about her.